Witch Is How The Drought Ended

Published by Implode Publishing Ltd
© Implode Publishing Ltd 2019

Chapter 1

"Just how dangerous will it be?" Jack had spent all morning worrying because it was the day of the Elite Competition.

I was pleased that he now knew my *big secret*, but at times like this, I wished he didn't. If I was to tell him exactly what was involved in the tournament, he'd be a nervous wreck.

"It's not dangerous at all," I lied. "It's just like a sports day really."

"But with dragons."

"There aren't always dragons."

"What if you get hurt? Or worse?"

"I won't, and besides, it's not like you have to spend all day worrying about me. I'll no sooner have gone than I'll be back again."

"Unless you've been eaten by a dragon."

"Dragons don't eat sups." Burn them to a crisp, maybe, but not eat them.

He took me in his arms. "Promise me you'll be careful."

"I promise." I gave him a kiss.

"What time are you going?"

"I might as well make a move now because I'm calling at Aunt Lucy's on my way to the Range."

"Are the twins going to the tournament?"

"No. They reckon they can't leave Lil and Lily because the guys are at work, but I think that's just an excuse. They both hate the Elite Competition, and I can't say I blame them."

"Who else will be there to cheer you on?"

"If previous tournaments are anything to go by, I

should have my fair share of supporters."

"And your grandmother, of course."

"Hmm. I could do without her. She'll be on my back all the time." I gave him another kiss. "Best get going. See you soon."

"Be careful."

Aunt Lucy and Lester were waiting for me outside their house.

"Morning, you two. The twins haven't changed their minds, then?"

"No, but they send you their best wishes."

"Is Grandma meeting us here?" I glanced next door.

"No. She popped her head in earlier to say she'd see us at the Range."

"We might as well get going, then."

"You seem remarkably calm, Jill."

"I am, but Jack's a nervous wreck."

"Jack?"

Oh bum! Once again, I'd failed to engage my brain before speaking. Aunt Lucy had no idea that Jack knew my secret. In fact, other than Daze and Blaze, no one else did.

"Err—yeah, he's got a big match today in the ten-pin bowling league. He's really nervous about it."

"For a minute there, I thought you meant—" She laughed. "Never mind."

***

The atmosphere outside and inside the Range was dramatically different to that of the Levels Competition.

The Levels attracted families, and had something of a carnival feel to it, but the Elite was a much more sombre affair. The tall, steel-mesh fence in front of the bleachers was there to keep the crowd safe from whatever horrors awaited the competitors.

"I thought you lot were never coming." Grandma tapped her watch.

"There's half an hour until the tournament starts," I said.

"Precisely my point. That's no time at all for our pre-tournament pep talk."

"Haven't we talked enough? I just want to get this thing over with."

"We'd better take our seats," Aunt Lucy said. "Good luck, Jill."

Before I could thank her, Grandma jumped in, "Luck has nothing to do with it." She grabbed my hand, and led me to one of the four cubicles provided for the competitors.

"Shall I get changed before we talk?" I said, once we were inside. I hated the traditional witch's outfit, which was provided for all competitors. It felt like some kind of ludicrous fancy dress costume.

"We can talk while you change." It wasn't so much a pep talk as a lecture, which pretty much went in one ear and out the other. "Did you get all of that?"

I hadn't heard a thing she'd said for the last five minutes.

"Yes. Every word."

"Good, and remember the most important thing is not just to win, but to humiliate Ma Chivers. By the time this tournament has ended, I want all of her supporters to realise just how weak she really is. Understood?"

"Absolutely."

"Competitors!" The voice came over the loudspeakers. "You will be introduced in three minutes."

"Make sure you remember everything we talked about," Grandma started for the door. "This is your chance to finish Chivers once and for all."

"Okay."

All alone in the cubicle, my thoughts turned to Jack. Although I'd be gone for no time at all, he'd still had all last night and this morning to worry. Curiously, I wasn't the least bit scared. That was probably a mistake because bad things can happen when you become complacent.

"Competitors, please show yourselves."

The four of us stepped out of our cubicles and lined up in front of the master of ceremonies.

"Ladies and gentlemen, welcome to this year's Elite Competition. I would remind you this competition can be very dangerous, and that the fencing is there for your protection. There will be wild animals in the arena, so under no circumstances should you try to scale the fence. With that out of the way, let's meet this year's competitors. On the far right, a previous winner of this competition, Martha Chivers!"

A small, but not insignificant section of the crowd, rose to its feet and cheered loudly. Leading the applause was none other than Cyril.

"Next, we have three competitors who are making their debut in the Elite Competition. First, please welcome Genevieve Gem."

Genevieve looked terrified, but managed to smile when

her supporters made themselves heard.

"Next to her, we have Roberta Rhinestone."

If anything, she looked even more scared than Genevieve, but she still managed a nervous wave to her supporters.

"And finally, someone who needs no introduction. Jill Maxwell is the first witch, below level six, to appear in this competition. I'm sure you'll all know the reason why that exception has been made. If you don't, where have you been for the last few years?" He laughed, and a large section of the crowd laughed along with him. Notably, Ma Chivers' supporters remained silent. "Please give it up for Jill Maxwell."

Modesty prevents me from mentioning that my supporters outnumbered the others by at least five to one.

The format of the competition was very simple: One competitor was eliminated in each of the first two rounds, leaving the remaining two to battle it out in the final.

My main memory of the Elite Competition was something that happened when I'd been a spectator. Grandma and Ma Chivers had played out a draw in the final. But it was what happened long after the tournament had finished that was etched on my mind. Back then, I wasn't nearly as powerful, so when I was confronted by a destroyer dragon, I'd thought my time was up. The only reason I'm still here today is that Grandma came to my rescue.

If the newspaper and TV news were anything to go by, this year's competition was a two-horse race; everyone expected to see Ma Chivers and me in the final. But if I'd learned one thing since I'd discovered I was a witch, it was to take nothing for granted.

"Ladies and gentlemen, the first round of this year's competition is all about *fire!*"

Oh bum! I hated spells that involved fire.

"The competitors will be required to use the 'burn' and 'fireproof' spells. *'Burn'* to attack their competitors, and *'fireproof'* to protect themselves."

This was precisely why I disliked the Elite Competition; it was unnecessarily dangerous.

"I know what you're thinking," the MC continued. "But there's no need to worry. None of the competitors need get burnt, provided they are sensible enough to retire when it gets too hot in the kitchen."

That was easy for him to say, but I wasn't convinced that the less experienced competitors would be capable of making the right decision in the heat of battle (definitely no pun intended). I couldn't in all conscience risk inflicting serious injuries on the other competitors—not even Ma Chivers. So, disregarding Grandma's instruction to take no prisoners, I decided I would use only the 'fireproof' spell—to protect myself. I had no intention of using the 'burn' spell to attack the others.

Ma Chivers had no such qualms, and set about attacking Genevieve and Roberta. They were both so overwhelmed by the assault that neither of them was able to go on the offensive because all of their energy was focussed on protecting themselves. It was upsetting to watch the two witches, cowering in front of Ma Chivers, and I was tempted to step in, but before I could, Jessica raised her hand to indicate that she'd had enough and wished to retire.

Although her supporters gave her a standing ovation,

she was obviously devastated at being eliminated so soon. On her way back to the cubicle, she whispered to me, "Good luck, Jill. Don't let Chivers win."

There was a break for a few minutes while they prepared the arena for the next round.

"What were you playing at?" Grandma appeared at my side. "Why didn't you use the 'burn' spell?"

"I'm not going to knowingly hurt someone unless I have to."

"How are you ever going to win with that attitude?"

"Mirabel Millbright!" the MC said. "No one is allowed on the field of play once the competition has started. I must ask you to leave immediately."

Before she did, she wagged her finger at me. "Stop messing around!"

Satisfied that Grandma had left the field of play, the MC continued, "Ladies and gentlemen, we come now to round two, which we have called simply: dragons. Those who have been to the Elite Competition before will be aware that the competitors can sometimes be required to face wild animals, including dragons. This year is no exception, but we do have something of a surprise for you today."

I didn't like the sound of that.

In between rounds, a number of fences had been erected on the field of play. I'd seen a similar set-up before, when I'd competed in the Levels Competition. The fences formed three separate lanes; each lane had a gate at one end.

The MC continued, "In a moment, I will ask the

remaining three competitors to enter their chosen lanes. Once they're inside, three lifts will deliver the dragons from the basement below the Range. The witch eliminated will be the first one to exit their lane. Unless of course, they're fried to a crisp or eaten first." The crowd gasped. "Only joking, folks." I wasn't so sure he was. I imagined the TV ratings would be through the roof if one of the competitors fell victim to a dragon. The guy was on a roll now, "I said that we had a surprise for you today, and I wasn't joking. Normally, competitors in this event are required to face the destroyer dragon, and for two of our witches, that will be the case. But something much more exciting awaits our third witch because, for the first time ever, we have a royal dragon."

The crowd were stunned into silence for a few moments, but then began to cheer loudly.

I didn't share their enthusiasm. "Wait a minute!" I shouted to the MC. "You can't do that! They're not called royal dragons; they're called conquestors, and they're nothing like destroyers. Conquestors are peaceful animals who simply wish to be left alone."

I might as well have been talking to myself for all the notice he took of me. He just ploughed straight on. "Competitors, please select your lane."

"Wait! This isn't right!"

My objections were in vain because Ma Chivers and Roberta went ahead and stood next to the lane of their choice.

"Three, two, one. Go!"

As my opponents had already entered the outer lanes, I had no option but to take the middle one. Hopefully, the conquestor dragon would be in my lane, and I'd be able to rescue it.

"Here come the dragons!" the MC yelled.

From below the ground, at the far side of the lanes, came the sound of the lifts rising from the basement. Otherwise, the Range was silent, as the crowd waited to see who would get the conquestor dragon.

It wasn't in my lane.

The ugly destroyer dragon took one look at me, and began to charge my way. I should have been afraid, but I was too concerned about the conquestor dragon. The solid fences were too high for me to see into the other two lanes, so I did the only thing I could: I levitated myself above the fence. From that elevated position, I could see that Roberta Rhinestone was staring at a destroyer dragon, which was racing towards her. Judging by the expression on her face, she'd be exiting through the gate at any moment. In the other lane, Ma Chivers was marching fearlessly towards the conquestor dragon.

"The use of levitation is strictly against the rules," the MC said. "Jill Maxwell is disqualified."

I didn't care about that. My only concern was to get to the conquestor dragon before Ma Chivers did. Fortunately, she hadn't realised I was in her lane, and by the time she did, I'd used the 'faster' spell to rush past her.

"Jill?" It was the conquestor dragon I'd encountered when trying to ensure safe passage for the CASS airship.

"Sybil?"

"I need to get back to Cora, but I can't fly."

Only then did I realise that her wings had been bound to her sides to prevent her from flying away.

"Let me get rid of these." It took all of my focus to find enough strength to break the bonds.

"That's *my* dragon, Maxwell!" Ma Chivers was charging towards us; she had a face like thunder.

I climbed onto Sybil's back. "Fly! Quickly!"

She didn't need telling twice. Moments later, we were airborne, and soaring above the Range.

"What happened, Sybil?"

"A flying creature came to the mountain. It looked a little different to the one that you'd asked me to leave alone, but I thought it would be okay. A few moments later, something hit me in the neck, and I began to feel groggy. The next thing I knew, I woke up in a dark room with my wings bound to my sides. Then, a few minutes ago, I found myself in that cage."

"When did they capture you?"

"Last night, I think."

"What about Cora?"

"She was fast asleep in the nest when I saw the flying creature. I hope she's alright. She'll have been scared if she woke to find me missing."

"What are we waiting for, then? Let's get back there."

"Are you coming too?"

"I might as well. I'm out of the tournament."

As Sybil sped home to the White Mountains, I held on for dear life. When the peaks were in sight, we began our descent.

"She's okay!" I'd spotted the nest. "It looks like she's still asleep."

Sybil seemed to speed up as we came into land, and I was terrified that I might get thrown off her back, but I managed to hold onto her neck.

"Kip, kip." Cora opened one sleepy eye. "Kip, kip."

"Thank goodness you're alright." Sybil put her paw gently on the baby's head. "You must be hungry."

"Kip, kip."

"I'm so sorry for what happened," I said, as Sybil fed the youngster.

"It wasn't your fault, Jill."

"If I hadn't asked you to leave the airship alone, you wouldn't have been so trusting of it."

"I won't be in future."

"I'll understand if you won't allow the airship to fly by from now on."

"The original flying creature has nothing to fear from me. It's already proved it means us no harm. But woe betide any others that come this way."

"That's very generous of you."

"Not at all. I may owe you my life because that creature, which was running towards us, looked like she meant to kill me."

"You could be right about that."

By the time I'd magicked myself back to the Range, most of the crowd had left.

Unfortunately, Grandma hadn't.

"What were you thinking?" she bellowed, after I'd changed back into my normal clothes.

"I couldn't allow them to hurt a conquestor dragon. They're peaceful creatures who wouldn't harm anyone."

"So you thought you'd throw the tournament and allow Ma Chivers to win?"

"What choice did I have?"

"You could have stayed and won. It's not like this is the first time that you've thrown a tournament either. Look what happened in the Levels Competition."

"The dragon was going to attack the crowd at the Levels. What was I supposed to do?"

"Always with the excuses. What was the point in me spending all that time preparing you for this competition?"

"I'm sorry, Grandma, but I couldn't allow Ma Chivers to kill Sybil."

"*Sybil*? You're on first name terms with a dragon?"

"We'd met before when I was helping the headmistress at CASS. She's really lovely."

"Do I look like I care about a stupid dragon?"
She didn't.

"I've already apologised. What else can I do?"

"Jill!" Aunt Lucy and Lester came rushing over. "Thank goodness you're okay. We were worried sick."

"Did you see what she did?" Grandma shouted. "She threw away her chance to beat Ma Chivers."

"But she's okay." Aunt Lucy gave me a hug. "That's all that matters."

"I give up!" Grandma stormed off. "You two deserve one another."

Chapter 2

"I still think there's something you're not telling me," Jack said while opening a new box of muesli.

"There isn't, honestly. Ma Chivers won; I lost. That's all there is to it."

"And there were no dragons at all?"

"I told you when I got back yesterday. They didn't have any wild animals this year. It was all very sedate."

"You seem to be taking this remarkably well, which isn't like you at all. Normally, you're a terrible loser."

"Rubbish. I'm always perfectly gracious in defeat."

"If you say so. I doubt your grandmother will be so gracious."

"Don't mention her. I'm going to lie low until she's got over it."

"How long do you think that will take?"

"No more than a year or two if I'm lucky."

"Is it today that you're holding the interviews for your office manager?"

"Yeah, this afternoon. I'm seeing them in Java's coffee shop."

"What's wrong with using your office?"

"Winky."

"Oh yeah." He laughed. "I'd forgotten your cat had his eye on that job."

"It isn't funny. Goodness knows how he'll react when he finds out that I've recruited someone behind his back."

"I used to think I had a lot to contend with at work, but my job seems like a breeze now, compared to what you have to put up with from that cat."

"No kidding. Winky is going to make my life a misery

once I drop the bombshell."

"Are you sure you won't change your mind about this weekend?"

Jack and some of his bowling buddies were going to Stroud for the weekend to watch the National Championships. He'd been trying to persuade me to go with him, but I'd rather pull my own teeth out without anaesthetic than spend two days with a bunch of guys talking non-stop about strikes, spares and splits.

"No, thanks. I'm going to have a lazy weekend all to myself."

"It'll be fun. Some of the other guys' partners are going."

"How many of them?"

"I don't remember exactly."

"Don't give me that. How many?"

"Just Liz. Henry's wife."

"I get it. The real reason you want me to go is so that Liz has someone to talk to. Not a chance. Are you forgetting I've met Liz before? She makes Mr Ivers seem interesting."

"What will you do stuck here by yourself all weekend?"

"I'll probably go into town and spend all your money."

***

When I arrived at the office building, I bumped into Jimmy and Kimmy on the stairs.

"How's it going, you two?"

"We've been at it all weekend, haven't we, Kimmy?"

"Yeah, but we're more or less done. All we need now are the signs."

"Did you speak to Mr Song?"

"I did." Jimmy rolled his eyes. "I see what you mean about his singsong voice. I found it rather off-putting at first, but he did give us a great price."

"And you remembered to mention about the fonts and positioning of the signs?"

"Yes, I emphasised all of that."

"I imagine you'll have a long wait?"

"Actually, no. He said he'd be able to fit us in straight away. He's going to install your sign and ours tomorrow."

"Oh? That's great." How come they got to jump the queue?

"Just in time for our open day on Wednesday," Kimmy said. "We've got ads running in the local paper and on the radio. You must drop by and take a look for yourself, Jill."

"I'll try to, but I do have rather a lot on this week. When do you actually plan on opening?"

"A week today."

"You must have tons to do, then. I won't keep you."

"Morning, Mrs V. I've just found out that our new sign is being installed tomorrow."

"Did Mr Song call you?"

"No, I heard it from those clowns next door."

"I'm not sure you should refer to them in that way."

"That's what they are, isn't it?"

"Yes, but it's the way you say it. Anyway, I have something important I want to ask you."

"As long as it doesn't involve clowns."

"It's about my niece, Dagmar. Her husband walked out on the family some years ago, and now she has to go into hospital for a few days. She's asked if I'd mind looking after her daughter, Angel, while she's in there."

"I assume you said yes?"

"Of course. I'm hoping that you'll allow me to bring her into work with me. She's a delightful child and not an ounce of bother."

"Wouldn't you rather take a few days off work and stay at home with her?"

"I considered that, but there's so little to do at my house for a youngster. I thought if she came here, she could use my computer. At lunchtime, I can take her into town to grab something to eat, and we can do some shopping."

"That's fine by me. How old is she?"

"Let's see. It's eight years since I've seen her, so—"

"Eight years? That long?"

"Yes, they moved away for several years, and they've only recently come back to Washbridge. She must be fourteen or fifteen by now."

"When will she be coming in?"

"Tomorrow, probably."

"I'll look forward to meeting her. Maybe I can talk to her about a career as a private investigator."

"I'm pretty sure that Dagmar wants Angel to have a *proper* career. A solicitor or a doctor—that sort of thing."

"Right." That had well and truly put me in my place.

"Oh, I almost forgot, a Jane Bond called a short while ago."

"Not *the* James—?"

"*Jane*, not *James*."

"Oh, right."

"She's coming in to see you in about thirty minutes. I hope that's okay."

"It is, and if the office manager interviews go according

to plan later today, you'll soon be able to check my schedule online."

"That sounds rather complicated."

"I'm sure it won't be. The office manager will show you how everything works."

Winky was curled up in the middle of the floor.

"What are you up to?" I said.

"Nothing."

"Don't give me that."

"I'm just lying here, minding my own business."

"Come on. I know you. What money-making scheme have you hatched this week?"

"I'm just being a cat."

"Hmm?"

I didn't trust him as far as I could throw him.

***

Jane Bond arrived five minutes early; she looked a little shaken. Winky was fast asleep when she arrived, and he didn't stir.

"Thank you for seeing me at such short notice, Ms Maxwell."

"Call me Jill, please. Would you like a drink?"

"No, thanks. I had one at a coffee shop just down the road. Strange place. Everyone kept shouting snap."

"That's Coffee Games. They have a different game theme every day. I usually stay away on snap day."

"I see. Before we start, do you mind if I ask one question?"

"Fire away."

"Why does it say clown underneath your sign?"

"That refers to the business just along the corridor: It's a clown school. Hopefully, by tomorrow, the sign situation will be resolved."

"I see. I thought it was a little strange. I'm here because my younger sister has gone missing. Her name is Pam. Pam Turton."

"How old is she?"

"Twenty-two. Three years younger than me."

"When did she go missing?"

"About two weeks ago."

"I assume you've contacted the police?"

"I have, but they're not interested."

"Given how long she's been missing, I find that rather surprising."

"When Pam was a teenager, she went through a difficult time at home. Our parents weren't the greatest. My father, in particular, was a difficult man to live with. I was just about able to put up with it, but he really wound Pam up. She ran away a number of times, for days at a time, but then she'd turn up again out of the blue. No one ever knew where she'd been. When I tried to file a missing person report, they brought up her record, saw how many times she'd run away in the past, and then seemed to lose interest."

"That's disgraceful."

"Maybe, but it's what happened. That's why I'm here."

"Was your sister having any problems? Relationships? Money? That kind of thing?"

"Not that I know of, but I hadn't seen her for almost a month. I'm afraid the last time we were together, we had a big argument."

"Is it possible that's why she left?"

"Definitely not. We often fall out, but we always have each other's backs."

"You said it was a *big* argument? Do you mind if I ask what it was about?"

"Not at all. Our father is very ill; he doesn't have much time left. I tried to persuade Pam that she should go and see him one last time."

"I take it that she didn't want to know?"

"She refused point-blank."

"Where does Pam live?"

"She has a houseboat on Washbridge canal. When she told me she was going to live there, I thought she'd lost her mind, but to be fair, she's turned it into a lovely little home. That's why her disappearance is so surprising. For the first time in her life, she has somewhere she can call her own."

"Does she live there with anyone?"

"No."

"She's not seeing anybody, then?"

"Not at the moment. At least, not as far as I'm aware. She was in a relationship, but they broke up about three months ago."

"What happened?"

"The guy dumped her."

"What about close friends?"

"Pam has always been a bit of a loner. As far as I know, the only close friend she has is Carly Broome."

"Have you spoken to her?"

"Yes, but she hasn't seen Pam for a while either."

"Even so, I'd like her contact details if that's possible?"

"Sure."

"Also, I'd like to see her boat if I can."

"Of course. I can meet you there and show you around if you'd like."

"Great. When?"

"I have to go straight to work after I leave here, and I daren't take any more time off this week. Maybe tomorrow evening, if that works for you?"

"That'll be fine."

On her way out, Jane glanced across at Winky who was now curled up on the sofa.

"That's a lovely cat you have there. I wish mine was as peaceful as he is. Toots runs around the house like something possessed, and is always scratching the furniture." She smiled. "I still love her, though."

Once Jane was out of the door, I turned to Winky. "This innocent act of yours doesn't fool me. I know you're up to something."

"I'm back!" Winky came in through the window.

Huh?

I glanced back and forth between the Winky on the sofa and the other Winky who was now sitting on the window sill.

"It's okay, Lionel," said the Winky on the window sill. "I've got this now."

"How do you put up with this one?" Winky, AKA Lionel, jumped off the sofa. "She's a bit much."

"I did warn you, buddy."

"Excuse me! I'm standing right here, just in case you hadn't noticed."

Lionel jumped onto the window sill, high-fived Winky, and then disappeared out of the window.

"You, Sir, have a lot of explaining to do." I fixed the

remaining Winky with my gaze.

"What do you want to know?" Winky jumped onto my desk.

"Who was that other cat for a start?"

"That was Lionel."

"I gathered that. I meant how come he looks exactly like you, and what was he doing here?"

"I thought you'd have worked it out by now. Lionel is a shifter."

"What?" I exploded. "Are you telling me I've been sharing my office with a strange man?"

"It's not like you've been getting naked in here or anything." He smirked. "Or have you?"

"Of course I haven't. How long has he been here?"

"Just since Saturday morning. Socks invited me over to his place, and we decided to make a long weekend of it. I knew you'd be worried if you came in today and found I'd gone, so I called Temporary Animals Inc."

"You've just made that up."

"No, I haven't. They provide temporary dogs, temporary rabbits, temporary chinchillas, temporary —"

"I get the picture."

"It's a brilliant business model. I wish I'd thought of it. A bunch of shifters got together and formed the company. If any animal needs to get away for a while they simply call Temporary Animals, and organise a replacement. Ingenious, eh?"

"Lionel didn't fool me. I knew something wasn't right about you — err — him."

"Yes, but then ours is a rather different relationship. Normally, the shifters supplied by Temporary Animals don't have to worry about holding conversations with their two-legged host. So, be honest, did you miss the *real* me?"

"Not in the least. It wouldn't have bothered me if you'd never come back."

"It's a good job I did. As part of a double act, you make a pretty good straight man, but as a solo act, you're pants."

"What are you talking about?"

"Just look back over these two chapters. Not so much as a guffaw until I came through the window."

"*Chapters*? Are you talking about the chapters of our lives?"

"You know what I'm talking about."

"And what's a guffaw?"

"It's the lowest rating on the laughometer, and you couldn't even manage that. Face it, Jill, without me, you just aren't funny."

"I don't have time for your nonsense. I have a business to run. The next time you decide to take a holiday, just go. I don't want any more creepy shifters in here."

"As you wish."

The cheek of that cat. Not funny? Me? That was just ridiculous.

And when I want your opinions, I'll ask for them. Which, just for the record, will be never.

After that shock to the system, I needed a cupcake, but I wasn't sure if I dared go to Cuppy C in case Grandma was there. She would no doubt have plenty to say about my performance, or lack of it, in the Elite Competition.

In the end, hunger got the better of me, and I decided to risk it.

"Is *she* here?" I said.

"Why are you crouched down there?" Amber peered over the counter.

"I'm hiding."

"I can see that, but why?"

"I don't want Grandma to see me."

"She isn't here. I haven't seen her for almost a week."

"Phew!" I got to my feet. "In that case, I'll have a caramel latte and a —"

"Blueberry muffin?"

"Actually, I quite fancy a cupcake. Strawberry, please."

"I heard what happened yesterday at the Elite Competition. I kind of wish I'd been there now — just to see Grandma's face when you flew off on that dragon." Amber laughed.

"I'm glad you think it's funny. She's going to make my life a misery."

"Why did you do it?"

"The idiots who organised the tournament had captured a conquestor dragon."

"I've never heard of those."

"Everyone calls them royal dragons, but their real name is conquestor. They're friendly creatures who wouldn't hurt a fly. I knew this particular one; she had a baby back home in her nest."

"Aww, poor thing. Was the baby alright?"

"Yes, thank goodness. Mother and child are both perfectly okay."

"That was a really nice thing for you to do, Jill. Giving up the chance to reach level six, and risking the wrath of Grandma, can't have been easy. I'm really proud of you."

"Does that mean I get these for free?"

"No chance."

It was worth a try. "How come you're here, anyhow? Aren't you and Pearl supposed to be off today?"

"Mindy lost a filling over the weekend, so I'm just covering for her while she nips to the dentist. Incidentally, Belladonna starts on Wednesday."

"The woman who's going to be working in the creche?"

"Yeah. You'll have to come over and meet her."

"I'll do that. It's a bit of a weird name, isn't it?"

"I kind of like it." Amber glanced around the shop. "If I tell you something, Jill, do you promise not to breathe a word of it to Pearl?"

"I don't like keeping secrets from either of you."

"It's nothing serious; just a bit of fun, really."

"Go on, then."

"It's the Candlefield Beautiful Baby Competition next week, and I'm entering Lil."

"That's great, but why wouldn't you want Pearl to know? I'm sure she'd like Lily to take part."

"I'm doing it to be kind, Jill. How do you think Pearl will feel when Lil carries off first prize and Lily doesn't even place?"

"Amber! That's a horrible thing to say."

"I know you have to be even-handed because we're both your cousins, but you know as well as I do that Lil is so much prettier than Lily."

"Hmm? What's the format of the competition?"

"You have to submit a photo by this Wednesday, and then the competition proper takes place on Saturday in Candlefield Community Centre. That's when the ten finalists are announced. Later that same day, the judges see the babies in person and select the winners. First prize is a voucher for Love Babies worth two-hundred and fifty pounds, and a trophy. You will come to the finals, won't you, Jill?"

"Err, yeah. I'll try to make it."

Chapter 3

I'd never had to go through the recruitment process before. Mrs V had been employed by my father long before I'd joined the business, and Jules had been interviewed over Skype by Winky. The post of office manager was a key position in the business, so it was essential that I chose the right person. The two candidates I was about to see both looked qualified on paper, so a lot would depend on the chemistry between us.

It was some time since I'd last visited Java's coffee shop. As I'd anticipated, the shop wasn't busy, so I was able to find a table at the back where we would enjoy some privacy.

The first candidate, Alistair Robinson, arrived a few minutes early. Full marks for punctuality, but deduct a point for the tartan suit. After we'd made our introductions, and I'd ordered him a cappuccino, we got down to business.

"I see you were born in Switzerland, Alistair."

"That's right. We lived there until I was thirteen."

"I guess that makes you the Swiss Family Robinson, then?" I laughed.

He didn't; he merely looked puzzled. "Sorry?"

"Your family name is Robinson, and you lived in Switzerland."

"That's correct." He still looked blank. Deduct one point for lacking a sense of humour.

"Never mind. Tell me, what made you decide to apply for this position?"

"I've always found office administration to be both challenging and fulfilling." I was tempted to dock him another point for being boring, but then I figured that was exactly what I was looking for in an office manager, and precisely why I wasn't cut out for the job. No one could ever accuse me of being boring. He continued, "I thought your business sounded fascinating, and would present me with a whole new set of challenges."

"That's very true. Perhaps it would help if I told you what I'm looking for in an office manager."

"Absolutely. Just a moment, please." He took out a small writing pad. "Do you mind if I make notes?"

"Err, no, please do. The main objective is to free up more of my time to spend on investigative work."

"Free up more time — check."

"I need someone to manage my diary, so that I know exactly where I should be and when."

"Manage diary — check."

"They'll also be expected to monitor expenses and payments received: cash and cheques."

"Cash and cheques — check."

"And to liaise with my PA, Mrs V."

"PA — check. Will your PA report to me?"

"Err, yes, I suppose so."

"Check. How many other employees do you have?"

"It's just me and Mrs V. And Winky, of course, but he's not actually an employee."

"Oh? Is he a contractor?"

"No, he's a cat."

"You keep a cat in your office?"

"Check — err, I mean, yes."

The next thirty minutes or so were taken up with a detailed discussion about his qualifications and experience, both of which were excellent. He also outlined his vision for my business. All in all, I was very impressed. Finally, we discussed the delicate matter of salary. His expectations were a little on the high side, but if I was able to spend more time on billable work, it shouldn't be a problem.

"Thank you very much for coming to see me, Alistair."

"My pleasure. When can I expect to hear from you?"

"By the end of the week."

"Excellent."

We shook hands, and he went on his way. Although I didn't want to pre-empt my final decision, the second candidate would have to be something very special to outshine Alistair.

I had ten minutes before the second candidate was due to arrive, so I took the opportunity to top up my coffee. Back at the table, I was making additional notes on the first candidate when I spotted a pair of tartan trousers headed my way.

Alistair was back, and he appeared to have taken off his jacket.

"Did you forget to ask me something?" I said.

"Sorry?"

"I thought maybe you'd forgotten to ask me a question."

"I'm a little confused. I'm here for the interview. You are Jill Maxwell, aren't you?"

Now, *I* was the one who was confused.

"I interviewed you a few minutes ago, Alistair."

"Don't tell me he has applied for the job too." He slumped down into the chair opposite me. "I don't believe it."

"Look, I have another candidate coming for an interview in a few minutes, so I'm going to have to ask you to—"

"Craig Robinson?"

"Yes. How did you know?"

"Because *I'm* Craig Robinson. Alistair is my twin brother."

"But you're wearing—" My gaze drifted down to his tartan trousers.

"The same clothes? That doesn't surprise me. Our parents insisted on dressing us alike until we were fourteen."

"*Fourteen?*"

"Ridiculous, I know. The result seems to be that we're almost telepathically connected when it comes to the clothes we wear."

"Do you live together?"

"Good gracious, no. We'd kill one another within a week. We live on opposite sides of Washbridge."

"Did you know your brother had applied for this position too?"

"I had no idea." He sighed. "I'm afraid this isn't the first time this has happened, but I suppose it's inevitable because we've both pursued an almost identical career path."

"I see. Well, I suppose we should get on with the interview if you're ready?"

"Absolutely. I'm raring to go."

One mark for enthusiasm.

"Your brother told me that you were born and raised in Switzerland?"

"That's right."

"The Swiss Family Robinson, then?"

"Sorry?"

His blank expression confirmed that neither of the brothers Robinson had a sense of humour. Minus one point.

The structure of the second interview was almost identical to the first, and many of Craig's responses matched those of his brother. Not only that, but many of his ideas and visions were the same. Even his salary expectations were similar.

"I think that's everything, Craig. Thank you very much for coming to see me today."

"My pleasure." He stood up and shook my hand. "When can I expect to hear from you?"

"By the end of the week, hopefully."

"Excellent."

Now I had a real dilemma. Both brothers had interviewed equally well, and there was nothing to choose between their qualifications and experience. How was I going to select the right man for the job?

As I walked back to the car, I was still wondering how I was going to choose between the two Robinson brothers.

"Jill! Yoohoo!" It was Deli. Her attire was always kind of left-field, but today, she'd surpassed herself. I owned belts that were wider than her micro skirt, and the boob tube looked as though it would give up the fight at any moment.

"Hi, Deli."

"I was planning to come to your office, but you've saved me the bother. I just wanted to apologise for sending you on a wild goose chase after that daughter of mine. I still can't believe she went sunning herself in Spain without a word to anyone."

In fact, the real reason for Mad's disappearance had been much more sinister. She'd been held against her will by one of the Dawson brothers, assisted by Mad's (now ex) partner, Simon Lister. Mad obviously couldn't tell her mother the truth, so she'd come up with the holiday story.

"No problem. I'm just glad she's okay."

"It's not as if she even managed to get herself a decent tan. I've seen her on Facetime, and she's as pale as a ghost. She'd have been better off having a spray tan. Cheaper too."

"As long as she's well rested."

"I guess so. Anyway, I have some big news about the salon."

"Oh?"

"We're introducing a brand new service that you may well be interested in." As she spoke, she seemed to be staring at my forehead. "Can you guess what it is?"

"I'm afraid not. You're going to have to tell me."

"Eyebrow threading."

"Isn't that a rather specialist service? You or Nails won't be doing it, will you?"

"Of course not. I've set on someone specially. Her name is Fifi La Soux — she has years of experience."

"Lasso?"

"Yes, La Soux. She's French." Deli's gaze drifted to my forehead again. "It looks like those caterpillars of yours could do with a bit of work. I'll give you a good discount, of course."

"Thanks. I'll think about it."

The first thing I did when I got into the car was to check

the rear-view mirror.

Caterpillars indeed!

***

Jack was already home by the time I got back.

"What do you think about my eyebrows?"

"Sorry?"

"What do they look like?"

"I—err—is this a trick question?"

"No. I just want you to tell me what they remind you of."

"They don't remind me of anything. They're just eyebrows."

"Are they too thick?"

"Err—no, they're—"

"Why did you hesitate? You think they're too thick, don't you?"

"No. They're absolutely fine."

"*Fine*? That's what people say when they don't like something, but are too polite to admit it. Do you think they look like caterpillars?"

He laughed. "Why would you think that?"

"That's what Deli said. Apparently, she's going to start offering brow threading at her salon."

"She's obviously just trying to drum up business. She's probably saying the same thing to everyone."

"Do you reckon?"

"Of course." He grabbed me around the waist. "Your eyebrows are perfect." He planted a kiss on both of them. "Just like the rest of you."

"You're not half bad yourself."

"By the way, did you notice next door?"

"What ridiculous costumes are Tony and Clare wearing this week?"

"No, I meant the other side. Monty's gone."

"Gone where?"

"I've no idea." Jack shrugged. "He's moved out."

"Are you sure?"

"Positive. The removal van was here this afternoon; it was just leaving when I got home. I tried to grab a word with him, but it was obvious he didn't want to talk to me."

"Do you reckon he's gone for good?"

"It looks that way. I had a quick peep through his front window after he and the van had left. The house looks empty."

"Poor old Monty."

"You hate him."

"I *don't* hate him. He drives me crazy, but that doesn't mean I wish him ill. What do you think has happened?"

"Your guess is as good as mine." As he spoke, Jack seemed a little distracted; he was staring out of the front window. "Did you see that?"

"See what?" I followed his gaze, but couldn't see anything; the street was deserted.

"That bush in what used to be the Makers' front garden."

"What about it?"

"I'm sure it just moved."

"It was a little breezy when I came in."

"I don't mean that it moved in the wind; it got up and moved from one side of the garden to the other."

"Have you been at that bottle of wine we opened

yesterday?" I grinned.

"I'm serious. It was over the other side of the garden a minute ago."

"Of course it was. Come on, let's order pizza. I reckon hunger is making you delusional."

I was done with Sloth Takeaway—life was too short to wait for them to make a delivery. Instead, I showed Jack the leaflet that had dropped through our letterbox a few days earlier.

"Pizza Pie?" He looked doubtful. "What kind of name is that?"

"It's actually quite clever if you think about it. On the one hand, it's a play on words: Piece of Pie—Pizza Pie. And also it describes perfectly what they do: they sell pizzas and pies. They have quite a selection—look on the back."

"I suppose it can't be any worse than Sloth."

"Shall we give them a try, then?"

"Yeah, go for it. I think I'll have the steak and kidney pie with chips."

I called the number on the flyer, and the phone was answered almost immediately.

"Pizza Pie. Pizza speaking. May I take your order, please?"

Pizza speaking? Okay, that was a bit weird, but at least they seemed on the ball, which was more than could be said for Sloth.

"Hi, I'd like to order a small margherita pizza, and a steak and kidney pie with chips, please."

"Anything to drink with that?"

"No, thanks. How long will it take? We're in

Smallwash."

"It should be with you in no more than twenty minutes."

"Great." I gave him the address and paid by card.

Fifteen minutes later, I was in the bedroom.

"The food's arrived." Jack shouted from downstairs.

I hurried down to find him still staring out of the front window. "I'll get the door then, shall I?" There was no response. "You just make sure that bush doesn't go anywhere."

"Pizza, pie and chips for Maxwell?" The delivery man was wearing a bright green uniform, which matched his van.

"Thanks." I took the food and gave him a small tip.

What? It was all the change I had on me.

"Hmm. Thanks." He started back down the drive.

"Just a second. I'm curious. How come when I rang, the man who answered the phone said, pizza speaking?"

"I get asked that a lot." He laughed. "It's not pizza; It's Pete Zah. That's the manager's name: Peter Zah. I keep telling him he should say *Pete speaking* or *Peter speaking*, but he takes no notice."

"Right, I see. Thanks again."

"I'm starving." Jack came out of the lounge and followed me into the kitchen.

"Has the bush moved again?"

"I didn't imagine it."

"Of course you didn't."

"I hope you remembered to tip the guy."

"I always remember to tip."

"No, you don't. I always have to remind you."

"Well, I remembered today, and a very generous tip it was too. You can give me your half later."

***

We'd just settled down for a night's TV viewing when there was a knock on the door.

"It's the fish man again." His van was parked out front. "How much more fish do you need?"

"He isn't due to come this week." Jack started for the door and I followed.

"Hi, Terry," Jack said. "I didn't think we were due a delivery this week."

"You're not. I just popped around to bring your free kippers."

"Oh?"

"Jill's sister has just placed her first order. That entitles you to a free pack of kippers for the referral." He handed them to Jack.

"Right, thanks."

"Couldn't we get the cash instead?" I asked. I'd never been a big fan of kippers.

"Sorry, Jill. It's strictly kippers only. Peter tells me he's something of a fisherman."

"So he says." Jack scoffed.

"I'm going sea fishing myself the Saturday after next. I asked Peter if he wanted to join me, and he seems very keen. You're welcome to come too if you like—there's plenty of room on the boat."

"Jack's not really a fisherman," I jumped in.

"I wouldn't say that," Jack said, defensively. "I used to go fishing occasionally when I was a kid."

"Since when? You never mentioned it to me."

"Are you up for it then, Jack?" Terry said. "Peter seemed to think you'd be too scared of the competition."

"Did he now? The last time I looked, he'd only ever fished on rivers. I don't think he's done any sea fishing, has he?"

"No, he said not."

"He'd still have an advantage over you," I said. "He has at least done some fishing."

"To be fair, Peter said as much, and offered to give Jack a five fish start." Terry grinned. "But he said that Jack would still be too afraid to take him on."

"Did he now?" Jack rose to the bait. "Well, we'll see about that. Sign me up, Terry."

"Nice one. I'll let Peter have the details early next week."

"What were you thinking?" I said, once Terry had gone.

"Didn't you hear what Terry said? Peter threw down the gauntlet."

"That didn't mean you had to pick it up. What is it with men?"

"You wouldn't understand."

"You're dead right I wouldn't. Peter goes fishing all the time. You don't know one end of a rod from the other. How do you expect to win?"

"This is sea fishing. Peter's never done that, so it will be a level playing field."

"What am I supposed to do while you go gallivanting around?"

"Why don't you spend the day with Kathy? You two hardly ever spend any time together."

"There's a reason for that."

Chapter 4

The next morning, I was in the lounge.

"Jack, quick! Come and see this!"

He came hurrying in from the kitchen, doing his best not to spill his muesli. "What's up?"

"Look over there!" I pointed down the street.

"What am I supposed to be looking at?" His nose was practically on the glass.

"That lamppost. It moved from this side of the road to the other."

"Ha, ha. You're hilarious."

"And that tree. That was a hundred yards up the road when we went to bed last night."

"I know what I saw: That bush over there definitely moved."

"Of course it did."

On my way out of the house, I bumped into Tony and Clare who were just about to get into their car.

"Has your other neighbour moved out?" Tony said.

"It looks like it. Jack said he saw the removal van here yesterday."

"Did you know he was leaving?"

"We had no idea. How come you two aren't in costume? Don't you have a con to go to this weekend?"

"No, thank goodness," Clare said. "After GiantCon, we're ready for a break."

"Tell Jill our news." Tony urged her.

"I thought we weren't going to tell anyone until we'd finalised everything?"

"Jill doesn't count."

"Thanks very much."

"Sorry, I just meant that you aren't part of the cosplay scene, so you can't spill the beans to anyone that matters." Tony was clearly bursting to tell me. "We've been involved with cosplay for some years now, and we got to thinking that maybe it was time to take it to the next level. We're giving serious consideration to running our own convention."

"I wasn't sure about it at first," Clare chipped in. "But Tony convinced me we could make it work."

"Isn't that rather ambitious?"

"It is, but we're confident we can pull it off. There's just one minor problem."

"The cost?"

"Well, yes, there's that, but more importantly, we have to come up with a theme. It can't be anything that's been done before, but it has to be something that will capture the imagination, and attract a large audience. I have to be honest, we've been racking our brains, but we haven't come up with anything yet. If you have any bright ideas, Jill, we'd love to hear them."

"Hmm? What about P.I.Con?"

"Too boring." Tony dismissed the suggestion out of hand.

"CatCon?"

"Been done."

"TortoiseCon?"

"That's pretty much already covered in TestudinesCon."

"TreeCon?"

"I'm not sure there'd be enough interest."

"I'll give it some more thought, and if I come up with

anything, I'll let you know."

***

Kathy's shop wasn't open, but I could see her in the back, so I knocked on the window.

"Morning." She let me in and then locked the door. "If you've popped in for a drink, you'll have to make it yourself. I've got a ton of things to do before we open."

"That's okay. I've not long since had breakfast. My crazy husband has just agreed to go on this sea fishing jolly with Peter."

"I didn't think Jack was into fishing?"

"He isn't, but he can't ignore a challenge, particularly when it's Peter who's thrown down the gauntlet. I tried to get him to see sense, but I might as well have talked to the wall. Anyway, I was thinking that you and I could go out for the day while those two are on the high seas."

"That's a great idea. I'm sure Pete's parents will have the kids."

"You can buy that meal you promised me."

"When did I promise that?"

"You said you'd buy me dinner because I helped you with the lease of your new shop. Remember?"

"I did say that, didn't I?"

"You can get me lunch instead. That's assuming you can make it on Saturday?"

"If Pete can spare the time to go fishing when he's as busy as he is, I don't see why I shouldn't spend a day with my sister."

"Peter's business is doing well then, I take it?"

"Yeah. Ever since he won that landscaping competition,

his feet have barely touched the ground. He's got at least a dozen big contracts to quote for, and he's holding interviews to try and recruit the additional staff he's going to need."

"As it happens, I was interviewing people yesterday too."

"Don't tell me you're still intending to go ahead with that crazy plan to bring in an office manager?"

"There's nothing crazy about it, and yes, I've seen two excellent candidates. The problem is I don't know which one to choose."

"If you can't decide between them, you'll have to toss a coin."

"I'm a professional. I don't make important business decisions based upon the toss of a coin."

"Did you notice the internet café when you came past?"

"No, I came the other way. Why?"

"It's closed."

"For good?"

"According to the notice on the door, yeah. Did your neighbour tell you that he was going to shut shop?"

"No, but then he moved out of his house yesterday. Without a word."

"Poor man. He hasn't had a lot of luck, has he?"

"He did win the lottery."

"Yeah, but there can't be much of that money left now."

"How's your new shop coming along?"

"Brilliantly. The shop fitters are already working on it. They should be done by the end of the week. I just need to find someone to run it for me. If you think of anyone, let me know."

"Will do."

Just as Kathy had said, the notice on the door of Have Ivers Got Internet For You, made it clear that the shop had now closed for good.

"Terrible, isn't it?" Betty Longbottom appeared in the doorway of She Sells. "The poor guy must be devastated."

"I guess so. How's your business doing?"

"Couldn't be better. The number of people visiting The Sea's The Limit is twice what I predicted, and of course, She Sells is feeling the benefit too. It's such a relief after the first misfire. I'm hoping that I'll have time to catch my breath now. I've been so busy, I can't remember the last time I got my hair done. And look at these nails. I'm ashamed of them. And don't even mention my eyebrows."

"Funny you should say that. Have you tried the new nail bar just down the road?"

"Nailed-It?"

"Yeah. The owner, Deli, is my friend's mother. I bumped into her yesterday, and she mentioned that they've just started to offer eyebrow threading. You might want to give them a try."

"Why not? They're certainly close enough. I might pop in there later today." Betty started back into the shop. "Thanks for the recommendation, Jill."

"Yes!" I punched the air in delight. "Thank goodness."

At long last, the signage situation had been resolved. Sid Song and his choirboys must have made an early start because my additional sign, and Jimmy and Kimmy's new sign, had both been installed. Thankfully, the Clown sign was in a different font and colour from mine, and the two signs had been positioned sufficiently far apart to avoid any possible confusion. It had taken way too long to sort out, but at long last, all was well.

I was so excited that I took the stairs two at a time, and then burst into the outer office.

"Mrs V, have you seen—?" I stopped midsentence because the person behind the desk wasn't Mrs V. "Who are you?"

The young woman with spiky purple hair had her feet up on the desk. Her back was to the door, so she hadn't seen me come in. She hadn't heard me either because she was wearing huge headphones—purple to match her hair.

I walked over to the desk and tapped her foot.

"Yeah?" She pulled one headphone away from her ear.

"Who are you?" I demanded.

"Who wants to know?"

"I do. I'm Jill Maxwell, and this is my office."

"I'm Legna." She slid the headphones down onto her neck.

Before I could ask any more questions, Mrs V came through the door behind me. "Jill, I see you've met my niece's girl."

"*This* is—?"

"Could I have a word in private, please, Jill?" Mrs V led the way through to my office and closed the door behind her.

"I'm sorry about this. I had no idea."

"What did she just call herself?"

"Legna. It's Angel backwards. Her mother says she refuses to respond to her real name. I can't believe the change in her; the last time I saw her, she was so sweet. I don't know how I'm going to cope."

"You'll be fine. Lots of teenagers go through this sort of stage. I'm sure that underneath all of — err — *that*, she's still the same sweet girl you used to know."

"I do hope so."

"Have you told her she can use your computer?"

"I did, but she just laughed. She said her phone was more powerful than that heap of junk."

"Nice." I could tell Mrs V was getting stressed, so I decided to change the subject. "Did you see that our additional sign has been installed?"

"Yes. Mr Song and his men were just finishing off when Angel and I arrived. It's much better."

"V! Hey, V!" Angel shouted from the outer office. "Is there anything to drink in this dump?"

Dump?

"She used to call me Auntie V," Mrs V said, wistfully. "Now, it's just V. I suppose I'd better see what she wants to drink."

"Who's that nutjob with the purple hair?" Winky said, once Mrs V had left the room.

"That's Angel. She's Mrs V's niece's daughter."

"She's got a right mouth on her."

"You and she should get on like a house on fire, then."

"I'll ignore that remark. Have you sorted out a time for my interview yet? I spent hours practising with Socks over the weekend."

"Err, not yet. I've had a lot on my plate. I'll let you know as soon as everything is sorted."

"Good. The sooner I take up the role of office manager, the better. I've got lots of ideas. Would you like to hear a few of them?"

"No." He looked crestfallen. "Better to save them for the interview."

"Okay, then. You're going to be impressed. I know you are."

Oh bum. This wasn't going to end well.

A few minutes later, Mrs V came through to my office. Angel followed her inside.

"Is it okay if I take Angel to—"

"It's Legna," Angel corrected her.

"Is it okay if I take *Legna* to the coffee shop? She won't drink ours."

"I only drink de-caff," Angel said. "And you don't have soya milk."

"Sure. I think it's Mouse Trap day at Coffee Games. You could have a game while you're down there."

"I don't want to play stupid games! I'm not a child!" She glanced across at Winky who was sitting on the sofa. "Cool cat. Why has he only got one eye?" She started towards him, but Winky was having none of it, and he bolted for the window. "Where did he go?"

"He probably heard one of his friends calling to him."

"What happened to his eye?"

"I don't know. It was like that when I adopted him."

"Poor little guy. Where does he live?"

"Here in my office."

"That must be really boring for him." She turned to Mrs V. "We should take him back to your place, V."

Unsurprisingly, Mrs V looked horrified at the idea. "Come on, Angel—err, Legna. Let's go and get that coffee."

No sooner had they left than my phone rang.

"Jill, it's Blaze. Are you busy?"

"Not particularly."

"Daze is in trouble."

"Why don't you pop over to my office so that we can talk?"

"I'd rather not do it there. Is there any chance you could come over to Candlefield? I'm in Cuppy C."

"Sure. I'll be straight over."

I'd half expected to find Daze with Blaze, but when I arrived at Cuppy C, he was on his own. Once we had our drinks, we found a quiet table where we wouldn't be overheard.

"What's going on? Where's Daze?"

"She's been suspended from all duties."

"Why? What happened?"

"She's suspected of covering for a sup who has revealed their identity to a human."

"You mean me."

"Shush!" Blaze glanced around, nervously.

"Sorry."

"A new boss has recently been appointed to head up the rogue retrievers. His name is Royston Rhodes, and between you and me, he's a nasty piece of work. He isn't interested in the welfare of the people working for him — only in making his mark and progressing his career even further."

"How does he know about me?"

"I'm not sure. He obviously doesn't have any proof, or he would have taken action by now. Against you and Daze."

Gulp.

Blaze continued, "The reason I didn't want to talk at your place is because I'm worried that Rhodes may have someone watching you. Have you noticed anything suspicious?"

"No, I can't say I—wait a minute—someone did plant a bug in my office the other day. He'd passed himself off as Mad's replacement, but I now know that wasn't true."

"That was probably one of Rhodes' people."

"What if I talked to Rhodes? I could try and explain that—"

"That would be the worst thing you could do. Until he actually has proof that Daze knows about you and Jack, there isn't much more he can do."

"Okay."

"You have to promise. I only wanted to make you aware of what was going on."

"I promise. I won't talk to your boss."

That didn't mean I was simply going to roll over and let this thing happen though.

Chapter 5

While I was in Candlefield, I decided to take a leisurely walk over to Aunt Lucy's. As I turned onto her street, I bumped into Pearl, pushing a pram.

"On your way to Mum's, Jill?"

"I am." I bent down to say hello to the little one. "Aren't you gorgeous?"

"She is, isn't she?" Pearl beamed. "I'm glad I've seen you, Jill. I have some exciting news, but you have to promise not to say anything to Mum, and especially not to Amber."

"I don't like keeping secrets from family."

"Neither do I usually, but I know Amber would be upset. Do you promise not to say anything?"

"Okay."

"I'm entering Lily into the Washbridge Beautiful Baby Competition. Obviously, she's bound to win, isn't she?"

"She's adorable, but there'll probably be lots of entries for a competition like that."

"But none as beautiful as Lily."

"Don't you think Amber would like to enter Lil?"

"I'm sure she would, but just think how upset she'll be when Lily comes first, and Lil comes nowhere. I'm being cruel to be kind."

"I can see that. Have you sent Lily's photo in yet?"

"How did you know we have to submit a photo?"

Oh bum!

"I—err—just assumed that was how these competitions worked."

"Right. Yes, I posted it yesterday. The final is on Saturday. You will come, won't you?"

"I wouldn't miss it for the world."

"Did you see Pearl and Lily?" Aunt Lucy asked when I walked into the lounge.

"Yeah. Lily is getting bigger."

"Both babies are."

"If I tell you something, do you promise not to say a word to either of the twins?"

"I don't like—"

"It's nothing bad, I promise. In fact, it's quite amusing."

"Okay, then. I promise."

I explained that the twins had both entered their little ones into the baby competition, but that neither of them knew the other had done the same.

"Oh dear." Aunt Lucy laughed. "They're both going to be in for a shock on Saturday. Do you mind if I tag along with you?"

"Not at all. I can't wait to see their faces when they realise. Naturally, they both assume that their daughter is going to take first place."

"Would it be awful of me to say that I hope neither of them does?"

"Yes." I laughed. "But that must mean I'm an awful person too."

"I'm glad you came over today. Do you think you could have a word with Rhymes while you're here?"

"Is something wrong?"

"He's down in the dumps because of that stupid poetry competition."

"I take it he didn't win, then?"

"He didn't even place in the top ten. He's barely spoken two words since then. Barry has tried to cheer him up, but it hasn't done much good."

"Okay. I'll go and see him."

The unhappy tortoise was on the floor in the spare bedroom.

"Hi, Rhymes."

He lifted his head slowly. "Oh, hello."

"Aunt Lucy tells me you didn't have any success at the 3T poetry competition."

"I've been deluding myself. I'm no poet. That competition confirmed it."

"That's nonsense. Competitions like that are very subjective. Just because one judge doesn't like your work, it doesn't mean—"

"There were three judges: a turtle, a tortoise and a terrapin."

"What I said still applies. Just because your work didn't speak to them, doesn't mean it isn't any good."

"I just want to see my poems in a book; that's all I've ever wanted. Now that's never going to happen. What's the point of continuing?"

"Come on, Rhymes. You can't give up just like that. Have you ever thought of publishing your work yourself?"

"I didn't realise you could do that."

"A lot of people do it, particularly in the human world."

"Could you help me to publish it?"

"Me? No, I wouldn't know how."

"It's never going to happen, then. I'll never see my work in print."

"I suppose I could try to do something, but it wouldn't be worth it until you have enough material to fill a book. I imagine that's going to take some time."

"No, it won't." He scurried (or at least, what passes for scurrying for a tortoise) over to a cardboard box. "This contains of all the poems I've ever written. There are hundreds of them."

"Right. Great."

"You're the best, Jill."

That's me: The best.

"What have you got there?" Aunt Lucy saw me struggling downstairs with the box.

"It's all of Rhymes' poetry."

"He hasn't asked you to burn it, has he? You can't do that."

"No, I sort of offered to get it published for him."

"Oh dear." She grinned. "How are you going to manage that?"

"I don't actually know, but the first thing I'll need to do is get it all on computer."

"Do you have time to do that?"

"No, but I know someone who does."

***

When I walked into the outer office, Mrs V shot me a puzzled look. "Jill? Where have you been? When we got back from Coffee Games, you'd disappeared."

"Sorry. I had to nip out for a few minutes."

"What's in the box?"

"I'm glad you asked. I'd like you to type these into the computer, please." I handed her the box. "It's for a friend."

"I had intended sorting out the client files; they're in a

bit of a mess. But if this takes priority —"

"I'll do it," Angel said.

"You?"

"I can type. Faster than you, probably. It'll cost you, though."

"Angel!" Mrs V shouted.

"It's okay, Mrs V. She's right. If she's going to work, then she should be compensated. How much?"

Angel walked over, took the box from Mrs V, and emptied the contents onto the desk. "Fifty quid."

"Twenty."

"Thirty-five."

"Thirty."

"Deal."

"Okay, but I'll be checking for accuracy."

"Fine by me." She shrugged. "You won't find any mistakes. Just one thing, though. I'm going to need payment in cash."

"No problem."

"Sweet. That can go towards the cost of the tattoo I've had my eye on."

***

I'd arranged to meet Jane Bond at six o'clock beside Washbridge Canal. Rather than try to describe her sister's boat to me, she'd suggested we meet at the bottom of the steps that led down from the Lock Keeper pub.

She was already there when I arrived.

"It's about a hundred yards this way." She led the way past a number of other boats, which were moored along the canal bank.

"I haven't been down here since I was a kid," I said. "My father used to bring my sister and me for a walk along the canal occasionally, but I don't remember there being so many boats moored here then."

"Boat living seems to have become more popular in recent years, probably due to the high house prices and rents around here. That's certainly what attracted Pam to it. That's it over there."

"The green one?"

"Yes. The Green Lady."

"It's much nicer than I was expecting. From the outside at least."

"You should have seen the state of it when she first took it on; it was a mess. Credit to Pam, though, she cleaned it up and gave it a lick of paint. The inside is even better."

"Can we get in there?"

"Yes, she gave me a key in case I ever visited when she wasn't here."

Jane stepped onto the boat and then turned back to me. "Watch your step."

"I'm not very good at getting on and off boats."

"Here, give me your hand."

The interior, although basic, was quite delightful, and certainly roomier than most of the bedsits I'd seen.

"She didn't have a lot of money to spend on it," Jane said. "Hence the lack of furniture. She was planning to add more as and when she could afford it."

"Is it okay if I take a look around?"

"Of course. Shall I wait on the towpath?"

"No, it's okay. It shouldn't take long."

After I'd finished looking around the main living area, I made my way to the bedroom, which was through a folding door at the far end of the boat. Inside, there was very little room for anything other than the bed.

"Jane!" I called her over. "Who's this man?" I held up the photo frame that had been on the narrow shelf next to the bed. The glass in the frame was cracked.

"That's Josh Radford. I mentioned him when I was at your office."

"Was he the guy who dumped her?"

"Yeah, she was pretty devastated at the time. I can't think why because from what she told me about him, he sounded like a complete loser."

"Would you happen to know where he lives?"

"Yes, I met Pam outside his block of flats once."

"Could you text me the address later?"

"Sure."

"Okay. I think we're done here."

"Hey!" A tall, red-faced man, wearing a lumberjack shirt, baggy trousers and knee-length galoshes was charging up the towpath towards us. "Is this yours?" He pointed to the boat.

"It belongs to my sister," Jane said.

"It needs moving, and it needs moving now."

"The owner isn't here to move it." I stepped in because I could see that Jane was intimidated by the man.

"That's not my problem. This is a short-stay mooring; it should have been moved three days ago."

I turned to Jane. "Is that correct?"

"Probably. Pam told me she couldn't afford a permanent mooring, so she moved to a different location every few days."

"So?" The man demanded. "What are you going to do

about it?"

"We've already told you that the owner isn't here," I said.

"And *I've* already told *you* that isn't my problem. If that thing isn't moved within the next two hours, I'll report it to the Canal Authority."

"Fine. I'll move it," I said.

"How are you going to do that?" Jane looked at me as though I'd lost my mind. "Do you know how to drive one of these things?"

"How difficult can it be?"

Very difficult as it turned out. Starting the engine proved to be easy enough, but the boat didn't seem to want to move. I couldn't for the life of me figure out why we weren't going anywhere.

"Aren't we supposed to undo those ropes?" Jane pointed.

"Well spotted. Can you get them?"

"Sure."

If I'd been thinking more clearly, I would have turned off the engine until Jane had released the ropes and climbed back on board, but I had a lot on my mind.

"Jill! Wait!"

I glanced around to see Jane, standing on the towpath, waving her arms around. Meanwhile, the boat and I were headed down river.

How come I could drive a car, but I was unable to steer the boat in a straight line? Still, I'd probably be okay just as long as I didn't meet anything coming in the opposite direction.

Oh bum!

The man piloting the other boat sounded his horn. As

the two boats came closer together, I could see him through the window; he was waving his arms around furiously. Another couple of minutes, and the inevitable would happen.

Unless.

I hurried onto the deck, grabbed a life-jacket, and then abandoned ship. The water was cold and murky, but the life-jacket kept me afloat while I cast the 'shrink' spell on the stricken boat. It was now small enough for me to pick up. Once I had it in my hand, I managed to half-swim, half-scramble onto the towpath.

The man in the other boat was staring in disbelief at what he'd just witnessed, so I quickly cast the 'forget' spell so that I wouldn't have to worry about him.

In the distance, I could hear Jane calling my name. I only just had enough time to put the tiny boat onto the canal, and restore it to full size before she appeared.

"You managed it?" She was trying to catch her breath. "I thought you were going to crash for sure."

"Nah, there's nothing to it." I tied the first mooring rope.

"You're soaked to the skin."

"I told you I wasn't very good at getting on and off boats."

***

Fortunately, Jane lived not too far from the canal, so she took me back to her apartment to dry off. She was also kind enough to lend me a change of clothes. Unfortunately, she was at least two sizes bigger than me.

"What on earth are you wearing?" Jack laughed. "And

what happened to your hair?"

"I fell into the canal."

"How did you manage that?"

"It's a long story. I'll tell you after I've had a shower."

"It's supposed to be your turn to make dinner."

"Do you think I threw myself in the canal just to get out of making dinner?"

"I wouldn't put it past you."

When I came back downstairs, Jack was on the phone, and it soon became obvious who he was speaking to.

"And I don't need a five fish start. Yeah, we'll see. You'll be laughing on the other side of your face. Okay, buddy, see you then."

"I take it that was Peter?" I said, once he'd ended the call.

"Yeah, he was trying his usual gamesmanship tactics to rile me, but it isn't going to work."

"Did I hear you say that you didn't want the five fish start he offered you?"

"Yes."

"Sounds to me like his tactics are working."

Chapter 6

The next morning, Jack and I had finished breakfast, and were enjoying a cup of coffee in the lounge when I spotted something out of the window.

"Jack, look! That bush moved!"

"This is getting really old."

"I'm serious. The one in the Makers' garden. I just saw it move from one side to the other."

He joined me at the window. "I've been trying to tell you that for days."

"I know you have."

"How about an apology for doubting me, then?"

"Let's go and see what's going on."

"I haven't finished my coffee."

"Fine, I'll go."

I didn't want to spook whoever or whatever it was, so I crept slowly across the road. When I was only a few yards away, the bush dashed back to the other side of the garden.

"Hey, you!" I charged towards it. "What are you up to?"

"Confound it!" Mr Hosey stood up. "You've blown my cover."

"Why are you pretending to be a bush?"

"After my re-election as chairman of the neighbourhood watch, I figured it was time to up the level of surveillance. That's why I bought Bramble."

"*Bramble?*"

"That's what I call this. It's very realistic, don't you think?"

"I guess so."

"Unfortunately, it's doing my knees no good at all. I think I might have been better off buying the tree."

"Where on earth do you buy stuff like this?"

"I got it online from Surveillance Foliage Supplies. They have a number of bushes and trees to choose from. The trees are awfully expensive, though." He glanced up and down the road. "I don't think anyone else has seen me. You won't give the game away, will you, Jill?"

"Of course not. Carry on bushing."

"Was that Hosey?" Jack asked when I got back into the house.

"Yeah. Apparently, this is all part of his new neighbourhood surveillance tactics. It seems he's beginning to regret not having bought a tree because all the kneeling is doing his knees in."

"It's not his knees he should be worried about; the man is insane."

"Tell me something I don't know."

"Are you going to apologise for having doubted me now?"

***

Oh bum!

I'd forgotten that today was Clown's open day. Someone had erected what looked like a miniature big top in front of my office building, so the only way I could gain access was through the tent.

"Welcome to Clown!" The clown standing by the entrance made his bow tie spin around. Hilarious. Not. "Straight up the stairs and turn left."

I couldn't be bothered to explain that I wasn't here for the clown school, so I took one of the leaflets he was handing out, and made my way through the tent and into the building. The queue of people on the stairs suggested that Jimmy and Kimmy had been correct about the level of interest. What surprised me most was the range of ages: from teens to a couple who were obviously in their seventies.

"Have you chosen your clown name, yet?" The young woman at the back of the queue asked me. "I thought I'd call myself Topsy. What do you think?"

"I don't really—err—"

"You don't like it, do you? Would Doodles be better?"

"I—err—"

"What about Twinkles?"

"Actually, I'm not here for the clown school. My offices are in this building too." I started up the stairs.

"What do you think of Popsy?"

I clearly wasn't the person to advise her on a matter of such importance, so I ignored her question and continued to fight my way up the stairs. Considering that the people in the queue were hoping to train as clowns, a few of them would need to change their attitude. Some of the comments hurled at me as I pushed past them were very un-clownlike.

"Just listen to this one, V." Angel was seated at Mrs V's desk.

Mrs V was sorting through the filing cabinet, and obviously hadn't seen me walk into the office. "You really shouldn't make fun of them, Legna."

"These poems of yours, Jill, are really—err—" It was all

Angel could do to suppress her laughter. "Very good. Aren't they, V?"

Mrs V looked around. "I didn't hear you come in, Jill."

"Just so you both know, those aren't my poems."

"Of course they aren't." Angel grinned. "We believe her, don't we, V?"

"Whose are they, then?" Mrs V asked.

"They belong to—err—I can't tell you that. The author wants to remain anonymous."

"I'd want to remain anonymous too if I wrote rubbish like this," Angel said. "Listen to this one. It's called The Sun."

"I don't think you should read—" Mrs V began, but Angel wasn't to be put off.

"The sun is big, yellow and very hot,
It's much better than rain; I like it a lot,
When the day ends, the sun says goodbye,
That's when Mr Moon takes over the sky."

Angel barely made it to the end because she was in tears of laughter.

"It isn't all that bad," Mrs V managed to say, but she too was on the verge of laughter.

"I've already told you. Those aren't my poems." It was obvious from their expressions that it was pointless trying to convince them, so I went through to my office.

"Whatever you do," Winky said. "Don't give up your day job. As a poet, you make a good taxidermist."

"Those aren't my poems. I'm just helping to get them published for a friend."

"Of course you are."

"It's true. If you must know, they were written by a

tortoise."

"You've been at those funny cigarettes again, haven't you?"

I'd had quite enough of this ridicule, so I magicked myself over to Candlefield library. I wanted to check the back issues of The Candle newspaper to see if I could find some information about the new man in charge of the rogue retrievers.

My tenure on the Combined Sup Council had been a spectacular failure. One of the many things I'd failed to achieve had been to persuade the council to allow the internet to be introduced in Candlefield. That meant, instead of being able to search online, I'd been forced to hunt through The Candle's dusty basement, which contained a million and one old newspapers.

It took the best part of an hour, and a thousand sneezes, but I managed to find a number of articles of interest. The most recent simply confirmed Royston Rhodes' appointment, but gave very little background on the man himself, other than to mention that he'd been working as a rogue retriever in London for several years prior to his promotion. Older articles mapped a spectacularly successful career. While in London, he'd recorded the highest number of 'arrests' of any rogue retriever. His numbers were nothing short of spectacular; twice as many as his closest rival. Based on that track record, there was little wonder he'd been promoted to head up the department.

I gave Blaze a call.

"It's Jill. Do you have a minute to talk about your new boss?"

"Sure. Where?"

"I'm in Candlefield. How about we meet in Cuppy C?"

"Okay. I'm just in the middle of processing paperwork for a rogue werewolf. Can we make it in twenty minutes time?"

"No problem. I'll see you there."

Pearl and Mindy were behind the counter.

"What happened to you, Jill?" Pearl said. "Are you okay? You're covered in dust."

"I've been searching the library's archives." I sneezed.

"I hear you have a tortoise poetry situation going on." She grinned.

"Yeah. Somehow, I managed to volunteer to help Rhymes to get his work published. I'm too nice for my own good, that's my problem." Pearl and Mindy exchanged an incredulous look. "What's that look about? It's true. I'm all give and no take."

"Of course you are. Anyway, how did your interviews for the office manager go?"

"Very well. I've seen two excellent candidates, but I'm not sure how to choose between them."

"If they're equally good, you'll just have to toss a coin."

"Why does everyone keep suggesting that? A professional businesswoman, such as myself, does not make decisions as important as this by tossing a coin."

"There's no need to bite my head off."

"Sorry. I'm having a bad morning."

Just then, several workmen came into the tea room.

"Why don't you pop upstairs, Jill?" Pearl said. "Belladonna started this morning. Go and introduce yourself. I'll have your coffee waiting for you when you come down."

"And muffin."

"That goes without saying."

The woman in the creche had her back to me; she was busy sorting through a pile of soft toys.

"Belladonna?"

She turned around. "That's me."

For some reason, I'd pictured her as an older woman, but despite her white hair, she appeared to be no older than me. Her dress sense was a little unusual, to say the least: A purple cape over a black dress, black tights with purple boots, and a black and purple ribbon in her hair.

"I'm Jill Maxwell. The twins are my cousins."

"They said you might be popping over today. They talk about you a lot."

"All bad, I assume."

"Not at all. They only have good things to say about you."

Now I knew she was lying.

"You must be looking forward to the creche opening next week."

"I am. I can't wait to see all the little darlings."

"I assume you've done this kind of work before?"

"I was a nanny for a few years. Since then, I've worked in a number of nurseries. I've always worked with young children; I love them. Do you have any kids, Jill?"

"No. I only recently got married. What about you? Do you have children of your own?"

"Not yet. Perhaps when I meet the right man."

"Where were the nurseries you worked in?"

"In the human world."

"In Washbridge?"

"No. Norwich, Leeds and London."

"You've certainly moved around a lot. What made you decide to come back to the sup world?"

"My mother isn't in the best of health, so I wanted to find a job back here in Candlefield to be near to her. This opportunity came at just the right time."

"Well, I hope you enjoy your time here. I'd better get back downstairs, there's a coffee waiting for me."

"And a muffin?"

Sheesh. Was there anyone in Candlefield who wasn't aware of my predilection for muffins?

Belladonna seemed nice enough, even if her taste in clothes left something to be desired. The tea room was still busy, so I collected my coffee and muffin, and took a seat next to the window.

"Hello, dearie." An old woman came and sat next to me, which was a bit weird given that there were several empty tables.

"Hi."

"I'm Fenella. Do you like parrots?"

Oh boy. "They're okay."

"I hate them. They're untrustworthy."

"Right."

"I could tell your fortune if you like?"

"I don't really believe—"

"There's no charge. It's free."

"I was going to say I don't really believe in that kind of thing."

"No one does, dearie, not until Fenella tells their fortune. Then they soon change their minds."

"Do you read palms?"

"Nah, I read muffins." She grabbed my half-eaten muffin, and stuffed it into her mouth.

I was so shocked that I didn't even react. Instead, I just watched her devour what was left of my muffin. When she'd finished, she brushed away the crumbs, and said, "You'll have a long and happy life."

"Fenella!" Pearl appeared at my side. "What have we told you about annoying our customers? Out you go!"

The old witch grumbled under her breath all the way out of the shop.

"What was that all about?" I said, after she'd left.

"She's a nuisance. She sneaks in here when we're busy."

"She reckoned she could see my future in my muffin."

"If you'd been eating a cupcake, she'd have used that. Basically, she'll say she can tell your fortune in whatever you happen to be eating at the time. Let me guess, you're going to have a long and happy life."

Blaze turned up a few minutes later. He didn't bother to order anything to eat or drink; instead, he came straight over to my table.

"How's Daze doing?" I said.

"You know what she's like. She makes out that she's not bothered, but I reckon this business has got her rattled."

"I did some checking on your new boss."

"In the library basement by the looks of it." He managed a smile.

"Yeah. From all accounts, Rhodes has had a spectacular career. The number of arrests he recorded in London was way higher than anyone else."

"So he keeps reminding us, but there's something not right about him. For a start, what kind of name is Royston

Rhodes for a rogue retriever? There's an unwritten rule that all rogue retrievers operating in the same region adopt rhyming names."

"Have you managed to speak to any of the people who were working alongside him down in London, to get their take on him?"

"Although he was assigned partners, he seems to have operated as a lone wolf. None of the other rogue retrievers could get close to him."

"What do you know about his personal life?"

"Not much, but there's bound to be information in his personnel file. I could try to get my hands on that."

"That's going to be risky, isn't it? What will happen if they catch you?"

"I'll be finished, but if that's what it takes to help Daze, then I'm prepared to take that risk."

***

After Blaze had left, I stayed on for a few minutes to finish my coffee. As I did, I heard a young woman crying. Pearl was seated at the table with her, obviously trying to comfort her. Moments later, Pearl walked her to the door.

"Is she okay?" I asked after Pearl had shown her out.

"That's Dabby. Amber and I used to go to school with her."

"She seemed rather upset."

"She works in Candlefield Zoo. Have you ever been there?"

"No, but then I'm not very big on zoos."

"You should go. As well as all the usual animals, they have lots of exotic species found only in Candlefield and the surrounding countryside."

"No dragons, I hope?"

"Definitely no dragons. The nice thing about Candlefield Zoo is that all the animals are kept in surroundings as close to their natural habitat as possible."

"So why was your friend so upset?"

"She's really worried about some of the animals under her care. It seems they've suddenly stopped drinking for no apparent reason."

"Are they ill?"

"She reckons not. They've been checked over by the vet, and he says they're in perfect health."

"If the vet says they're okay, I'm sure everything will be alright."

"That's what I was trying to tell Dabby, but the poor girl is inconsolable."

Chapter 7

I magicked myself back to Washbridge, and made my way to my office building. Clown's open day was still going strong, so I once again had to enter through the big top.

The same clown made his bow tie spin again—it was even less funny the second time around. As I walked past him, he offered me a flyer.

"It's okay. You gave me one earlier."

"Back again already? You must be keen."

"Like you wouldn't believe."

The queue on the stairs had disappeared, but there were still lots of people hanging around the corridor between my office and Clown's. I was just about to go into the office when I heard footsteps heading towards me. I turned around to find a young man being pursued by a woman of a similar age; she appeared to be holding something.

"Don't!" The man stopped a few feet in front of me, and then turned to face his pursuer. "Please, Julie! Don't!"

"You had this coming." She laughed as she threw what I now realised was a custard pie at her boyfriend.

The young man's reflexes were amazing, and certainly much faster than mine. He ducked down, so that the custard pie flew over his head.

"I'm so sorry," the young woman said. I could hear her, but I couldn't see her because my eyes were full of custard pie. "That's your fault, Tommy. You shouldn't have ducked."

"Are you alright, lady?" the young man enquired, nervously.

"I'm great. Absolutely great." I wiped the gunk from my eyes.

"Is there anything we can do?" The young woman offered.

"I think you've done enough."

As soon as I walked into the outer office, Angel dissolved into laughter.

"I'm beginning to like it here," she said. "You didn't tell me that Jill was so funny, V."

"Are you alright, dear?" Mrs V walked over to me. "What happened to you?"

"I've been custard-pied."

"Oh dear. Can I do anything?"

"No, it's fine." I stomped off towards my office.

"You should write a poem about it, Jill," Angel shouted after me.

"Oh boy!" Winky was next to break into hysterics. "What happened?"

"What does it look like?"

"It looks like you were eating a custard pie, and missed your mouth, but I know that can't possibly be right. Not with the size of your —"

"Are you tired of breathing?"

"I could lick it off for you if you like."

"Don't be so gross." I grabbed a box of tissues and started to wipe my face clean.

"I'm glad you're back." Winky jumped onto my desk. "I wish to register a complaint."

"And you thought *right now* would be a good time to do it?"

"That woman out there is a nightmare."

"You've already made it very clear that you don't like Mrs V. What's new?"

"Not the old bag lady. That niece of hers. Angle or whatever her name is."

"It's Angel not angle. And she isn't her niece; she's her niece's daughter."

"That's just grand, but she's still a nightmare."

"What has she done to annoy you?"

"She keeps coming in here, wanting to play with me."

"What's wrong with that?"

"I have much more important things to do than 'play'. I'm in the middle of negotiations for my autobiography."

"What do you expect me to do about it?"

"This is your office. Kick her out."

"Trust me, I'd love to, but I can't. I promised Mrs V that she could come with her to the office for a few days."

"Jill." Angel came charging into the room. "Have a word with V, would you?"

"About what?"

"She says I can't get a tattoo. What's the point in my typing all of your stupid poems if I can't use the money to get inked?"

"I've told you. They're not my poems."

"Whatever. Will you tell V to let me have a tattoo?"

"I'm not getting involved. You'll have to sort it out between you."

"Fine!" She stormed out of the room.

"Hey," Winky said. "I could do her a nice tatt. It wouldn't cost her much either."

***

When I left the office, Mrs V and Angel were obviously still not speaking to one another. Before I left the building, I called in the cloakroom to give my face a wash because although I'd managed to wipe off the gunk, I could still smell it.

"Jill!" Someone called to me when I came back out.

"Jimmy. How's the open day going?"

"It's Breezy when I'm on duty."

"Sorry, I forgot."

"It's going much better than we could have hoped. There was a queue for most of the morning. A lot of people have signed up for the school already. You should pop in and take a look."

"I'll try to, but I'm on my way out at the moment, and I'm not sure if I'll make it back into the office again today."

"If you do manage to come and see us, I should warn you that there are a lot of custard pies flying around."

***

The Washbridge Canal Authority is a kind of police force, which monitors activity on the canals. Their offices were close to The Lock Keeper pub.

"Hello, young lady." The jolly little man was chewing on a stick of liquorice, which had stained his mouth black. "Would you care for a piece?"

"No, thanks."

"I swear by the stuff. Keeps me regular."

"Nice."

"Probably not something you need to worry about at

your age, but trust me, when you're as old as I am, you'll view it differently. I'm Norris. Norris Morris."

"Nice to meet you, Norris. I'm Jill."

His fingers were also covered in liquorice, so it came as something of a relief when he didn't offer to shake hands.

"How can I help you, Jill?"

"I'm trying to trace a young woman who's gone missing. She lives on the boat called The Green Lady."

"I know the one. Made a good job of renovating it, she has. And you say she's missing?"

"Yes. Her sister is very worried; that's why she contacted me. I should have mentioned that I'm a private investigator."

"Well, well, well. If you'd asked me to guess, I'd have said you were a florist. You have the look of a florist."

"I was wondering if you have CCTV of the towpath around this stretch of the canal."

"Indeed we do, but unfortunately I'm not able to show it to you. The only people who can make such a request are the police. Are they looking for the missing woman?"

"I'm afraid not. Are you sure you couldn't bend the rules just this once?" I gave him my sweetest smile.

"Sorry. It's more than my job's worth. Are you sure you wouldn't like some liquorice?"

"No, thanks. Just one last thing, could you tell me if there's much crime around here?"

"Usually no, but there have been a couple of burglaries recently."

"Boats?"

"Yes."

"I don't suppose you could tell me which boats they were?"

"I shouldn't really, but I don't suppose it would hurt."

***

I was in no mood for any more of Clown's open day, or for Angel, so I'd more or less decided to go home when I got the phone call I'd been dreading.

"Hi, Grandma."

"Where are you?"

"Near Washbridge canal."

"What are you doing?"

"I was thinking of calling it a day and going home."

"Would you mind popping over to Ever for a few minutes first, please?"

"Err—yeah, okay."

"Thank you."

After she'd hung up, I stared at the phone in disbelief. Was I hallucinating, or had she just asked *if I'd mind*, and said *please* and *thank you*? It had to be some kind of trick. She was clearly lulling me into a false sense of security, so that once I was down there, she could let me have both barrels. But what could I do? I'd just said I'd go, and besides, I was going to have to face up to it sooner or later, so I might as well get it over with.

Julie, the head Everette, was wearing the new yellow uniform.

"Have you got used to that yet?" I said.

"What do you think? How would you like to have to walk around looking like a canary?"

"What kind of mood is she in?" I gestured to Grandma's office.

"She was in a foul mood on Monday morning; she bit

everyone's head off."

"Did she mention my name by any chance?"

"She did, but nothing I'd like to repeat."

"That bad?"

"Worse, much worse, but then yesterday, she seemed to calm down a little."

"And today?"

"I couldn't really say. I haven't seen that much of her. She was already here when I arrived."

"I suppose I'd better go and face the music."

"Good luck."

I took a deep breath and knocked on Grandma's office door, half-hoping she might be asleep and not hear me.

"Come in!"

"Hi, Grandma."

"Have a seat, Jill. Would you like a drink? I can get Julie to rustle something up."

This was killing me. She was obviously toying with me, like a cat playing with a mouse before the deadly strike.

"No thanks, I'm okay. Look, about what happened at the Elite—"

"That's done and dusted. No point in raking over those old coals now."

"Really? Right, I couldn't agree more."

"What's the point? You don't have the killer instinct, and nothing I could say is going to change that."

"I wouldn't exactly say—"

"So, to the reason I asked you to come over. You already know I'm the chairman of W.O.W, I believe?"

"Witches of Washbridge? Yes."

"I'd like to formally invite you—"

"To join? Thank you, Grandma. I didn't think you'd ever —"

"Not to join. I want you to give a talk to the ladies on growing up as a human."

"Hang on. Are you saying that even though I'm not good enough to join W.O.W, you'd like me to give a talk to them?"

"Correct. Next Wednesday morning at ten o'clock sharp."

"What exactly do you want me to talk about?"

"I've just said, haven't I? Some of our members have only recently moved to the human world. And even some of those who have been here for a while have limited experience of humans. If you ask me, that's a good thing, but they seem to feel it would be beneficial to get a better insight into how humans think."

"But I'm not a human."

"I realise that, but you're the closest thing we have. I can hardly invite a real human to give the talk, can I? So, you'll be there?"

"I guess so. Where is it?"

"In our new custom-built HQ: W.O.W. Central. Take the north road from the marketplace, and keep walking. You can't miss it."

"How long would I be expected to speak for?"

"If it was up to me, I'd say no more than thirty seconds, but I expect the ladies will feel short-changed with anything under twenty minutes."

"How did it go?" Julie caught me on the way out.

"Better than I expected. I think."

***

Jack's car was already on the drive when I got home.

"Did you see?" he said, as soon as I walked through the door.

"See what? Hosey hasn't gone and bought himself a tree, has he?"

"No. I meant next door; the new neighbours have moved in."

"Already? Monty only moved out at the weekend."

"They're renting it; that's how come they've moved in so quickly."

"You've spoken to them, then?"

"Yeah, just before you came home. They seem nice enough: Britt and Kit."

"*Britt* and *Kit*? Seriously?"

"Yeah. Britt and Kit Lively. They have the most beautiful white cat."

"Another cat? That's all I need."

Chapter 8

The next morning, I was at the kitchen table, trying to muster the energy to keep both eyes open. I could manage one at a time, but two would have taken too much effort.

"Look out here!" Jack was staring out of the kitchen window.

"I'm too tired to move. We don't have moles again, do we?"

"No, it's the new neighbours. They're both exercising on their back lawn."

"Are they insane? Don't they know what time it is?"

"I'm going out to talk to them. You should come and introduce yourself."

"Looking like this? No, thanks. I can't speak to anyone until I've had coffee and a slice of toast."

By the time Jack came back inside, I'd refuelled on caffeine, and was feeling marginally more alive.

"Apparently, Kit works in a gym."

"That's nice for him."

"And Britt is a personal trainer."

"Why are they working out in their back garden if they're going to be doing that kind of stuff all day?"

According to Britt, it's important to warm up before they start work for real."

"Freaks."

"They seem really nice. They got me thinking." I already didn't like the sound of this. "We've been saying that we should find some kind of hobby or interest that we could share."

"So?"

"This could be it. We're both a little out of shape."

"Speak for yourself, buddy."

"Not drastically, but you can't deny we should do more exercise than we do."

"I kind of enjoy the exercise we already do together."

"So do I." He grinned. "But we could do more. Kit said we were welcome to give his gym a trial for free for a month, and Britt says she has a few slots free."

"I hope you didn't commit us to anything?"

"No, I said I'd talk to you about it. Don't you think it would be a good idea?"

"I don't know. I tried to get into an exercise regime at I-Sweat, but I never seemed to find time."

"Yeah, but if we did it together, it would be fun. We'd be exercise buddies. What do you say?"

"I'll have to think about it."

"Okay." He checked his watch. "I'd better be making tracks. I have a briefing first thing this morning." He gave me a kiss. "See you tonight. And give some thought to what I said."

"I will." For all of thirty seconds.

When I'd envisaged a shared hobby or interest, I'd imagined something sedate—something that would allow us to relax after a busy day at work.

This definitely wasn't it.

How come Jack never thought to empty the kitchen bin? It didn't matter how full it was, he always managed to squeeze a little more rubbish inside, rather than have to take the bag out to the bin.

I did a quick check through the window to make sure the new neighbours weren't still pumping iron in the back garden. The last thing I needed was to have to listen to them extolling the benefits of exercise.

The coast was clear, so I tied the black sack and headed around the back of the house. I'd no sooner dumped it in the bin when—

"Hi!" The female half of our new next-door neighbours suddenly popped up; she must have been doing some kind of exercise below the level of the fence.

"Oh? I didn't realise you were still out here."

"I'm Britt. You must be—err?"

"Jill."

"Of course. Kim has an early start today, so he had to cut his session short. I've still got another ten minutes to do."

"Right. Jack said that you're a personal trainer."

"I am. I absolutely love it. I used to work at the same gym as Kit; that's where we met. I started my own business about a year ago. What do you and—err—sorry, I'm terrible with names."

"Jack."

"Of course. What do you and Jack do? We didn't get a chance to ask him."

"Jack is a policeman; he works in West Chipping. I have my own P.I. business."

"How very exciting. You must have to keep super fit for that kind of work?" She looked me up and down. "Don't you?"

"Of course, but it's not always possible to find the time."

"It needn't take too much time if you use it wisely. Did your husband, err—"

"Jack."

"Did Jack mention that Kit had offered a free trial at his gym?"

"He said something about it, but he had to rush off."

"I have a few slots available too. I could have you back in shape in no time at all."

Back in shape?

Just then, a snow-white cat jumped onto the fence between us, and began to sashay back and forth, meowing at the top of its voice.

"I haven't forgotten you." Britt stroked the needy cat. "Do you like cats, Jill?"

"I have one back at the office; his name is Winky."

"That's an unusual name. This is Lovely."

"Yeah, it's been great."

"No." She laughed. "That's the cat's name: Lovely."

***

When I arrived at the office, I feared the worst. The battle of the tattoo would no doubt still be raging between Angel and Mrs V; I just hoped they didn't expect me to adjudicate.

But I needn't have worried because the two of them were chatting like long-lost friends.

"Morning, Jill." Mrs V was all smiles.

"I've finished typing these." Angel handed me the box. "I've called the document: Jill Maxwell's Poems."

"They aren't my—never mind. Thanks."

"Have you got my money?" She held out her hand, at which, Mrs V shot her a disapproving look.

"I'd like to take a quick look at what you've done before I pay up."

"Fair enough, but you won't find any mistakes."

"What are you going to do with the money?"

"I won't be getting a tattoo." She sighed. "V saw to that."

"I spoke to Legna's mother last night," Mrs V said. "She was well enough to take my call, and she's forbidden Legna from getting a tattoo."

"Yeah, but she said I could get those DMs I've been after for ages instead. She's going to put the rest of the money towards them. V and I are going to get them at lunchtime, aren't we, V?"

"We are." Mrs V seemed relieved that the two of them were back on speaking terms.

"Why don't you come with us, Jill?" Angel said.

"Err, thanks, but I've got a ton of work on today."

"Did you know that new shop of your neighbour's has closed down, Jill?" Mrs V said.

"Yeah, but he isn't my neighbour any more. He moved out at the weekend."

"Poor man. Do you know where he's gone?"

"No idea. He left without a word. When I got home last night, our new neighbours had moved in."

"That was quick."

"They're renting, apparently. They're both keep-fit nuts, and they have a cat, Lovely."

"Well that's just dandy!" Winky didn't look happy.

"What's wrong with you?"

"I'm not happy."

See, what did I tell you?

"What's up? Has your autobiography deal fallen through?"

"Of course not. All the big publishers are fighting for the rights to it."

"So why the face?"

"I heard what you just said about the lovely cat."

"That's not what I said. I said they have a cat and her name is Lovely."

"And is she?"

"Is she what?"

"Lovely?"

"She's just a cat."

"Hey, watch what you're saying. There's no such thing as *just* a cat. Is she a looker?"

"She was very well turned out."

"What colour fur does she have?"

"White. Snow white."

"I love snowies. When do I get to meet her?"

"You don't. I've already explained that I'm not allowed to have cats under the terms of my lease."

"How come your next-door neighbour has one, then?"

That was a very good question. Think, Jill! Quickly!

"It's quite complicated. I'm not sure you'd understand."

"Try me."

"It's all to do with the leases. The property owners are forbidden from keeping cats, but when a property is rented, the terms of the rental agreement may allow it."

He thought about that for the longest moment, and I was beginning to think I'd got away with it when he said, "That doesn't make any sense. Legally speaking, you can't override the terms of the lease by the terms of a subsequent rental agreement. Any good lawyer will tell you that."

I shrugged. "I only know we're not allowed to keep

cats. I'm really sorry. You know I'd love to take you home with me if I could."

"Hmm."

***

Halfway through the afternoon, I had an unexpected visitor: Reggie, the caretaker from CASS.

"I hope you don't mind my dropping in unannounced like this, Jill. I won't take up much of your time."

"Not at all, but I am rather surprised to see you here in Washbridge. Is everything okay?"

"That remains to be seen."

"Take a seat. Can I get you a drink?"

"No, thanks. I've heard a lot about that coffee shop on the high street—the one that has game themes. I thought I might pop down there afterwards."

"It's called Coffee Games."

"That's the one. I heard it's Jenga day today. I love that game. Do you play it yourself, Jill?"

"Not really. In all honesty, I'm not much of a board game fan. You were saying it remains to be seen if everything is okay?"

"Sorry, I got distracted. Ms Nightowl has now left the school, and the new headmaster has taken up his post."

"Cornelius Maligarth? What do you make of him?"

"I've had virtually no contact with him, but he's already upset a lot of the other staff. Philomena Eastwest has taken early retirement."

"Why? What happened?"

"I'm not sure. She wouldn't go into detail, but after she'd had a one-to-one in his office, she said she'd never been spoken to like that in all of her years in teaching. I'm fairly sure some of the others would like to leave too, but they have families to support, so it isn't that easy."

"I'm really sorry to hear that. It's such a shame after the fantastic atmosphere Ms Nightowl had cultivated."

"The reason I came over here today, apart from the Jenga, of course." He grinned. "Is because Maligarth has been asking about you. He seems really keen to speak to you. I thought you should be forewarned."

"Thanks. I appreciate the heads-up. My next lesson isn't until next Friday."

"I have to come back to Candlefield next Thursday evening, so I'll be travelling back first thing Friday. We could travel together if you like?"

"On the airship?"

"How else would we—oh yeah, I'd forgotten—you can magic yourself there, can't you?"

"I can, but I'm happy to go on the airship with you. We can have a nice chat on the journey over. Do you have any idea what the headmaster wants to talk to me about?"

"No, but every time he mentions your name, he—err, maybe, it's just my imagination."

"Go on. What were you going to say?"

"His eyes seem to turn bright orange. But, like I said, I probably just imagined it."

***

Jane Bond had given me the address for Pam's ex-boyfriend, Josh Radford. He lived in one of the tallest and oldest blocks of flats in Washbridge. At the time it was built, back in the seventies, Wash Point was thought of as a masterpiece of nouveau architecture. Now, it was considered an eyesore that was well past its sell-by date. It was only a matter of time before it was demolished, but for the time being, a few unlucky residents were still forced to live there until such time as they were rehoused.

Josh Radford lived on the top floor of eight, and wouldn't you just know it, both lifts were out of order. By the time I reached his flat, I was beginning to think that Jack might have been right about my being out of shape.

All I needed now was for him not to be home; that would put the tin lid on it.

Fortunately, he answered after the first knock. Judging by the size of the plaster on his chin, he must have been shaving in the dark.

"Josh Radford?"

"Yeah. Are you okay? You look terrible."

"The lifts are both out of order."

"I very much doubt it." He grinned. "That'll be the Wise kids."

"Sorry?"

"Gary and Barry Wise. They get a kick out of sticking the 'Out of Order' signs on the lifts."

"You mean they're actually working?"

"More than likely. They were definitely working earlier."

"Great. My name is Jill Maxwell. I'm a private investigator. I'd like to ask you a few questions about Pam Turton."

"She and I haven't been together for several months."

"So I understand. You dumped her I believe?"

"I wouldn't say dumped, exactly, but I did end it. She was too needy. Is she alright? Has something happened to her?"

"She's gone missing."

"Did you know she did that a lot when she was a kid? Run away, I mean."

"Yeah, her sister told me. I'd like to ask you a few questions if I may."

"I was just on my way out. I have to get to the job centre or I'll lose my benefits."

"Can we talk while you're walking?"

"Sure." He led the way over to the lift, and as he'd predicted it was working just fine.

"I believe you and Pam lived together for a while?"

"Yeah, for about four months."

"Did you both live here?"

"Yeah."

"When did you last see her?"

"When I told her it was over."

"Have you ever been on her boat?"

"No. She didn't get that until after we'd split up. I only know about it because one of her friends told me."

The lift doors opened on the ground floor. "I have to run, or I'll be late, and those idiots at the job centre will stop my money."

Chapter 9

Back at the office, Angel was wearing her new DMs.

Mrs V had some too.

"What do you think, Jill?" Mrs V's spindly legs looked even thinner than usual with the huge boots on her feet.

"Green?"

"Legna said green was my colour."

"They're very nice. Can you actually walk in them, though?"

"They're going to take a bit of getting used to."

"What do you think of mine, Jill?" Angel had gone for the classic black.

"They're great. I'm sorry I haven't got around to checking the work you did yet."

"That's okay. V lent me the thirty-pounds, so you'll need to let her have it once you're happy with what I've done."

"Fair enough. I'll check the document as soon as I'm at my desk."

When I went through to my office, Winky was lying on his side on the sofa.

"What are you doing?" I said.

"I'm not feeling so great."

"What's wrong?"

"I don't know. I just feel out of sorts."

"Have you had anything different to eat? You haven't been scrounging food from somewhere else, have you?"

"No, it's not that. I've only eaten what you've given me."

The poor little guy didn't look at his best.

"Take it easy and see how you feel later."

Without another word, he climbed gently off the sofa, and disappeared underneath it. That cat drove me crazy most of the time, but I hated to see him like that.

Before I loaded the document that Angel had created, I changed the file name to 'Rhymes'. Although I only skimmed through it, I discovered two things: First, Angel was a remarkably accurate typist—I didn't find a single mistake in any of the poems I checked. And second, Rhymes was a truly awful poet.

What? I know he's a cute little tortoise, but as a poet, he stinks big time.

While I was paying Mrs V the money I owed her for Angel's work, Blaze came into the outer office.

"I've got it, Jill." He held up a blue file, triumphantly.

"Great. Come through to my office."

"Where's your cat?"

"He's under the sofa; he's not feeling very well."

"Poor little guy."

"Did you have any trouble getting hold of this?"

"Not really. I'm quite friendly with one of the women who works in H.R." He gave me a knowing wink.

"Sly old you."

"She's no more enamoured with Rhodes than the rest of us. She gave me the nod when her boss was going to be out of his office for a few hours."

"Won't the file be missed?"

"This is a copy." He handed it to me. "I had a quick skim through it. There isn't very much in there, but I did spot the names of two of his ex-partners in London."

"I thought he worked as a lone wolf?"

"He was assigned partners, but it seems he effectively ignored them, and did his own thing. Still, it might be worth having a word with them. It's possible they could have something on him that would help."

"You're right, but if I contact them, is it likely to come back and bite you?"

"I wouldn't have thought so. I've yet to speak to a rogue retriever who has a good word to say about him. And anyway, that's a risk I'm prepared to take."

"Have you seen Daze?"

"No. I didn't want to contact her again until I have some good news for her."

On his way out of the office, Blaze glanced under the sofa. "I hope you're feeling better soon, old guy."

The very fact that Winky didn't respond to being called an *old guy*, made me think he really must be under the weather.

***

Mid-afternoon, I received a phone call from a number I didn't recognise.

"Jill, it's Butter."

"Hi. Thanks for the flowers—they were beautiful."

Princess Buttercup, AKA Butter, ruled over the floral fairies. A recent crop failure had caused them to resort to stealing flowers from the human world. When I'd realised that the floral fairies were behind the thefts, and confronted the princess, she'd taken full responsibility, but she'd also explained the situation, and promised that it wouldn't happen again. I could see she'd been placed in an impossible position, so I'd decided not to take the matter any further.

"Jill, I'm sorry to call you out of the blue like this, but I don't know who else to turn to."

"What's happened?"

"I don't suppose you could come and see me, could you?"

"Sure, I'll pop over straight away."

"Thanks, Jill. I really do appreciate it."

After magicking myself over to Hyacinth House, I shrank myself and made my way into reception where Heather Meadows was waiting for me.

"The Queen is expecting you."

"Queen?"

"Yes, her majesty decided it was time to accept her rightful title."

"That's great news."

Heather showed me to the queen's private office where Butter was on the phone; she gestured for us to enter while she continued her conversation, "I'm really sorry to hear that, Pippa. You'll be sorely missed. Please keep in touch. Okay, bye." When she finished on the call, she turned to us. "Thank you, Heather. Will you have drinks sent through, please? What would you like, Jill?"

"Tea would be nice. Milk and one and two-thirds sugar, please."

"I'll see to it straight away." Heather left us alone.

"It's nice to see you again, Queen Buttercup."

"Please don't call me that." She blushed. "I'm sorry to have kept you waiting. That was the manager of Candlefield Flowers, one of our best customers."

"I didn't realise you supplied shops too. I thought you

only delivered direct to customers."

"We do both. Seventy/thirty in favour of direct sales. If there were more shops of the quality of Candlefield Flowers, we'd probably do more through the shops. I just hope whoever they get to replace Pippa is half as good."

"Is she retiring?"

"Good gracious, no." Butter smiled. "Pippa is only a young witch. She recently met a human and is moving to the human world to live with him. As you can imagine, she's rather nervous."

"Does she have a job to go to?"

"Not as far as I know."

"If she's as good as you say she is, I may be able to help her there. My sister is just about to open a new shop and she's looking for someone to manage it. It's a bridal shop."

"I'm sure Pippa would be interested. In my dealings with her, I've always found her to be first class, and I'm sure her current employer will confirm that."

"I'll mention her to my sister and see what she thinks. Incidentally, how come you changed your mind about taking on the title of queen?"

"That was partly your doing. You convinced me that I was ready to accept the title, but more importantly, my people deserve to have a queen. Even so, I'd prefer it if you still called me Butter."

"As you wish, your majesty." I grinned. "You sounded rather desperate when you phoned me earlier. What's wrong?"

Before she could answer, Heather brought through the tea and a selection of enticing fairy cakes.

Butter deliberately waited until Heather was out of the room before explaining the reason for her call. "I don't want word to get out; it could cause mass panic."

"That sounds bad."

"It is. You may recall that I told you we'd opened up a number of new plantations to ensure we weren't crippled by crop failure again?"

"Yes, it sounded like a solid plan."

"It is, or at least, it should have been."

"What's gone wrong?"

"We've just discovered that we're experiencing the same problem at all of our new plantations."

"By the *same problem*, do you mean a water shortage?"

"That's right. We were very careful when choosing the location for the new plantations. We deliberately sought out regions that had local water supplies to provide the necessary irrigation. And yet, within no time at all, the water supplies in all of those areas have started to dry up. It doesn't make any sense because the rainfall has been average or even above average for the time of year."

"What do you think is happening?"

"I honestly don't know, but I'm beginning to suspect foul play of some kind. That's why I contacted you. I'm hoping you'll be able to get to the bottom of it. That's if you have time to help us?"

"I'll make the time. I don't want you to find yourself in a position of having to raid the human world again."

"No matter what happens, we won't do that. I gave you my word, and I don't intend to go back on it."

"Where do you suggest I start?"

"I think you should meet our plantation manager, Thistle Patch. He'll be able to show you around all of the plantations, so you'll be able to see for yourself what's happening."

"Excellent. When can I do that?"

"Thistle is on holiday this week, but he'll be back on Monday if that works for you?"

"Monday will be fine."

"I'll send you a text with the details nearer the time."

"Okay, and don't worry, Butter. I'll get to the bottom of this."

"I really do hope so, Jill."

***

"I think there's something wrong with the cat," Mrs V said, as soon as I got back to the office.

"Why?"

"Legna put some food out for him, but he hasn't touched it. That's not like him. He's usually wolfed it down before I have the chance to get out of the door. Do you think he's okay?"

"He's been a bit off it all day."

"Are you going to take him to the vet?"

"I think I'll take him home with me and keep an eye on him. If he deteriorates, I'll take him straight to the vets."

Winky was still very subdued, and didn't say a word when I put him into the cat basket. Again, that wasn't like him because he normally hated going into that thing.

When I pulled onto the drive, I realised there was something different about Tony and Clare's front garden, but it took me a few seconds to realise what it was. Then it struck me: that tree hadn't been there in the morning. Leaving Winky in the back seat of the car, I went over to take a closer look.

"Is that you, Mr Hosey?"

"Drat, you're good, Jill." A small slot opened in the bark. "How did you know?"

"It wasn't really that difficult. There wasn't a tree here this morning, and now there is."

"But you have to admit it's realistic."

"Maybe too realistic. Just watch out a dog doesn't decide to pee on you."

That had him worried. Snigger.

I carried the cat basket into the lounge, and gently lifted Winky out. He still seemed pretty much out of it, so I put him on the rug.

"Would you like anything to eat?"

He shook his head.

"A drink?"

"Water, please."

After I'd placed the bowl at his side, I left him alone. Maybe he'd sleep off whatever it was that was ailing him.

"Hi, beautiful!" Jack arrived home twenty minutes later.

"Shush!" I beckoned him into the kitchen.

"What's wrong?"

"I've got Winky in the lounge."

"The cat? I thought you said you'd never bring him home?"

"The poor guy's not very well. He's been under the weather all day, so I thought I'd better bring him home with me in case he deteriorates overnight."

"Can I go and see him?"

"No, let him sleep. That's what he needs right now."

"Okay. Incidentally, when did Tony and Clare get that

tree planted?"

"Please tell me you're joking?"

"Didn't you see it? Sheesh, Jill, I thought P.I.s were supposed to be observant."

"Of course I saw it, but I also realised it was actually Mr Hosey in one of his surveillance disguises."

"Are you sure? It's very realistic."

Oh boy!

We'd just finished dinner when there was a knock at the door.

"I'll get it." I hurried to see who it was.

It was Kathy; she had Mikey with her. I ushered them both into the kitchen.

"I've got Winky in the lounge."

"Can I go and see him?" Mikey said.

"Not today. He's a little poorly."

"What's wrong with him?" Kathy asked.

"I don't know. He's been listless all day, and he's refusing his food, which isn't like him at all."

"Poor little thing."

"He'll probably be okay by morning, but if he isn't, I'll take him to the vets. Now, what brings you two here?"

"Mikey has something to ask you, don't you?"

"Auntie Jill, I have to get someone to come to my school to talk about their job, and I'd like you to do it, please."

"Oh? What about your mum and dad?"

"We both volunteered," Kathy said. "But, according to Mikey, our jobs are too boring. He said he wanted you to do it because you have a cool, exciting job."

"That's very true."

"Please, Auntie Jill. None of the other kids have any

relatives with a job as good as yours."

"Okay. When would I have to do it?"

"Are you sure about this, Jill?" Kathy said. "It'll be quite nerve-racking standing in front of a classroom full of kids."

"Of course. I already teach every other week."

"What?"

Kathy looked totally confused, and there was little wonder. I'd done it again; I'd opened my mouth before engaging my brain.

There was no way to talk myself out of that gaffe, so I was forced to cast the 'forget' spell on both her and Mikey.

"Are you sure about this, Jill?" Kathy said again. "It'll be quite nerve-racking standing in front of a classroom full of kids."

"I think I'll be okay. I can only do my best."

"It's next Tuesday afternoon," Mikey said.

"I'll be there."

"Say thank you to Auntie Jill," Kathy encouraged him.

"Thanks, Auntie Jill. You're the best."

"No problem." I turned to Kathy. "I was going to call you later. I may have found someone for the manager's job in your new shop."

"Who's that?"

"Her name's Pippa and she comes highly recommended. She's been managing a flower shop but is looking for a new challenge."

"Great. Tell her to give me a call and we can arrange an interview."

"Will do."

After they'd left, Jack had a huge grin on his face.

"What's tickling you?"

"You almost dropped yourself in it then."

"I forgot I couldn't talk about CASS in front of them."

"What would you do without that 'forget' spell of yours? I bet you used to cast it on me all the time before I knew you were a witch, didn't you?"

"I forget."

Chapter 10

I sat up in bed with a start.

It was one in the morning and, needless to say, Jack was still sleeping like a baby. What had woken me? I remembered hearing a familiar voice: Winky's voice. Had it been a dream or was he calling to me from downstairs? Maybe he'd taken a turn for the worse?

I jumped out of bed, dashed out of the bedroom and down the stairs — two at a time.

"Winky, are you okay?" I burst into the lounge — half-expecting the worst.

There was no sign of him.

Perhaps he'd been feeling sick, and had made his way to the kitchen so as not to make a mess on the carpet. He could be considerate when he tried.

"What's going on?" Jack was halfway down the stairs.

"I thought I heard Winky."

"Is he sick?"

"I think so, but he's not in the lounge. He might have gone through to the kitchen."

Once Jack had joined me, I gently pushed open the kitchen door — dreading what I might find.

"Where is he?" Jack glanced around the room.

"I've no idea."

Just then, I heard a voice coming from outside: Winky's voice.

"Was that him meowing?" Jack said.

"Shush!" I put my finger to my lips. "He's talking to someone. Let me listen."

"That's right, Lovely. A private investigator. Of course, I practically run that business. My two-legged is pretty useless.

I'm not sure what she'd do without me."

"That's very interesting, Winky. I'm one of the top feline models in Washbridge. You've probably seen some of my work."

"I may have. I've helped to crack some high-profile cases. There was the – "

"I did the Catkins campaign. You must have seen that one. It was all over the magazines."

I beckoned Jack to follow me out of the kitchen, and back up to the bedroom.

"He must be feeling better," he said.

"Feeling better? He was never ill in the first place. It was all just an act."

"That's a bit harsh. He looked terrible earlier."

"That's what he wanted us to think. I can't believe I fell for it."

"Why would he pretend to be ill?"

"Why do you think? He'd heard me talking about Lovely."

"Lovely what?"

"That's the name of next door's cat. That's who he's talking to out there."

"I could only hear them meowing at each other."

"Think yourself lucky. It was nauseating."

"What are we going to do? Should we bring him back into the house?"

"I don't trust myself. If I get my hands on that cat, I'll strangle him. He can stay out there with his lady friend."

"What about tomorrow?"

"I've no doubt he'll continue with the dying swan act, but it's not going to wash. He's going back to the office."

***

The next morning, I woke earlier than usual; Jack was still sound asleep.

Winky would no doubt be back in the lounge, continuing with the charade, in the hope of spending another day at the house. Well, let me tell you, that devious cat was in for a very rude awakening.

"Morning, Jill." Winky was sitting on the rug. "What a beautiful morning it is."

That totally threw me. "I suppose you're still feeling poorly?"

"No, I feel terrific." He jumped to his feet. "Never better. Shall we get going?"

"Hold on. Are you saying you want to go back to the office?"

"Absolutely. I can't wait to get back there. I'm looking forward to seeing the old bag lady and Angle."

"It's Angel. What are you up to?"

"Me? Nothing. I'm back to my old self and looking forward to going home."

"I know you were faking yesterday. It was all just an act to get me to bring you home with me, so that you could chat up Lovely."

"Guilty as charged."

None of this computed. Why was he so keen to get back to the office? And why had he so readily admitted that the previous day's supposed illness had been nothing but an act? Colour me confused.

"I don't get it, Winky. What's going on? Why are you so keen to get back to the office, and why did you confess so easily?"

"If I tell you, do you promise to take me back this morning?"

"Okay. I promise."

"When I heard you talking about Snowflake next door, I thought she sounded like the kind of hottie I usually go for."

"And you put on the dying swan act, so that I'd bring you home?"

"Correct. I was good, wasn't I? If there were Oscars for—"

"Never mind that. Why the sudden change of heart this morning?"

"I got talking to Snowdrop last night."

"I know. I heard you."

"I wish you'd brought me back into the house. That cat could bore for England. All she wants to talk about is her wonderful modelling career and her beauty regime. She's a keep-fit fanatic too. Did you know that?"

"I didn't, but having seen the neighbours, it doesn't surprise me."

"I couldn't get a word in edgeways. It took me all my time to get away from her."

Now, everything made sense. "You're still looking a little peaky. Maybe, you should spend another day here. I could always ask the neighbours to look after you." I started for the door.

"You're joking, right? You wouldn't really make me spend a whole day in the company of that boring cat, would you?"

"What was it you said about me last night when you were talking to Lovely? That I was *pretty useless*?"

"That was just a joke. You know that, right? Jill, come back! Jill!"

Snigger.

Ten minutes later, Jack joined me in the kitchen. "Where's Winky?"

"In the lounge."

"Is he okay?"

"Physically, yes, but he isn't a happy bunny."

"Why? Because you're taking him back?"

"Quite the opposite, actually. He's having a meltdown because he thinks I'm not going to take him into the office this morning."

"I don't get it. I thought he'd try and wangle another day with Lovely."

"Apparently, Lovely isn't so lovely after all. According to Winky, all she wants to do is talk about herself. That's a big no-no as far as he's concerned because all *he* wants to talk about is *himself*. He confessed that he'd pretended to be ill, and begged me to take him back to the office this morning."

"So why aren't you?"

"I am. I don't want him spending another night under this roof, but I'm going to enjoy watching him suffer for the next few minutes."

"Remind me never to cross you."

***

"How is he?" Mrs V asked, as soon as I walked through the door. "How's the cat?"

"He's fine." I held up the basket for her to see.

"I've been worried about him all night. What was it?"

"It must have been some kind of twenty-four hour bug." I put the basket on the floor, and let him out.

What followed was a sight that I never thought I'd see. Mrs V was stroking Winky while he weaved in and out of her legs, purring.

"Where's Angel?" I said.

"They discharged her mother a day earlier than expected, so she returned home last night."

"You must have been sorry to see her go?"

"I know I shouldn't say this, but I was quite pleased to see the back of her. I can cope with them when they're little, and all they want to do is play. I don't really understand teenagers."

"You and ninety per cent of the parents in the country." I started for the door. "Come on, Winky."

He followed me through to my office, and jumped onto the sofa. "It's good to be back home."

"It's nice to see you and Mrs V are BFFs."

"Hmm, I wouldn't go that far. Let's just call it a temporary truce."

"How temporary?"

"What time is it?"

"Nine-thirty."

"It just ended."

***

I'd arranged to meet with the Trumans. Theirs had been one of the boats that had been burgled recently. Unlike Pam Turton, the Trumans had a permanent mooring, which was half a mile downstream from where the Green Lady had been moored at the time of Pam's disappearance.

"You have a lovely boat," I said, as Mr Truman helped

me on board.

"Thank you. Doris is below deck. Shall we join her?"

I followed him down the steps into the main living area.

"Jill, I'm Doris. I've just put the kettle on. Would you prefer tea or coffee?"

"Whatever you're having is fine by me."

While Doris went to the kitchen area to make the drinks, I settled down on one of the bench seats.

"I'm Tommy, by the way." He took the bench seat opposite me.

"What's the story behind the boat's name?"

"Can't you guess?" He grinned.

"High Kicker? Not really. You're going to have to give me a clue."

"Doris!" he shouted. "Jill can't guess why we called the boat High Kicker."

Moments later, she brought the tray of drinks over and put it on a small table. Then, she took a few steps back and said, "This might give you a hint."

She was a small, slim woman of at least sixty-years of age, so when she suddenly kicked one of her legs as high as her head, I was somewhat taken aback. There was no way I could ever have managed that.

"I've still got it." She beamed. "Although, to be honest, doing that once a day is enough at my age."

"You were a dancer?"

"Not any old dancer," Tommy chimed in. "She was on the West End stage, weren't you, Doris?"

"In my prime, but that's a long time ago." She joined her husband on the bench seat.

"The people at the Canal Authority told me that yours was one of the boats to be burgled recently."

Their expressions suddenly became much more solemn; the incident had obviously had a lasting impact on them.

"We're seriously thinking of giving her up," Tommy said.

"The boat? How long have you lived here?"

"Almost fifteen years," Doris said. "And to be honest, we thought we'd be here until ill health forced us back on land, but the burglary has made us have a rethink."

"You mustn't let some lowlife chase you out of your home. What did they take?"

"Nothing that can't be replaced." Tommy took his wife's hand in his. "It isn't what was stolen; it's knowing that someone was in our home."

"They trashed it, you know." Doris was struggling to hold back the tears. "It wasn't necessary. They could have taken what they wanted and left."

"You'd never know it had been trashed, now." I glanced around.

"Our family helped us to get it cleaned up again, but it still doesn't feel the same."

"Where were you when the burglary took place?"

"We'd gone to stay with our daughter for a few days. We'd had such a lovely time, but then we came back to—" Her words trailed away.

"What do the police have to say about it?"

"They came to take our statements, and said they'd let us know if there was anything to report, but I got the impression that they're inundated with this kind of thing."

"I didn't notice any CCTV cameras close by."

"No. There are some a little further upstream, but none that cover the boat." Tommy finished the last of his coffee.

"You said you were investigating a missing person? How is that connected to our burglary?"

"It probably isn't, but I have to explore all possible avenues. The people at the Canal Authority mentioned there had been a number of burglaries recently, so it's always possible that Pam — that's the missing woman — that she disturbed a burglar."

"You don't think that burglar might have killed her?"

"Hopefully not. It's quite possible that there's a more innocent explanation, but as I said, I need to cover all bases."

Doris and Tommy both saw me off the boat.

"I'm hoping to talk to another boat owner who was burgled. I've phoned her a couple of times but didn't get any response. You don't happen to know where I can find a boat called No Mornings, do you?"

"That's Suki's boat," Doris said. "Suki Coates; she lives by herself. We're good friends with her; we often visit each other's boat for a cuppa." Tommy pointed downstream. "Her mooring is a five-minute walk from here, but you won't find her there today. She's holidaying somewhere in France this week. She should be back on Sunday, I believe."

"Late Saturday night, actually," Doris said.

"Okay, I'll try and catch her when she gets back. Thanks again for your time, and I hope you change your mind about giving up this lovely boat."

***

Back in Washbridge, I decided to call in at Coffee Games. The Trumans were a lovely couple, but their coffee left a lot to be desired. I needed a real caffeine hit to get me through the rest of the day.

When I approached the counter, there seemed to be no one serving. I was just about to call for service when Sarah jumped up, scaring me half to death.

"Sorry, Jill, did I make you jump?"

"Just a bit, yeah."

"It's hide and seek day. It's the first time we've tried this, and to be honest, I'm not sure it's working."

"Who were you hiding from?"

"Andy. He's the other barista."

"Right, but don't you have to stay behind the counter?"

"Yeah."

"It's not going to be too difficult for him to find you, then, is it?"

"I know. Like I said, I'm not sure this was such a good idea."

"Got you, Sarah!" A man appeared at my side. "I've been looking everywhere for you."

Oh boy.

Chapter 11

I was beginning to think that the people who owned Coffee Games were losing the plot. It was one thing to play board games, but the move to games like hide and seek was, in my not so humble opinion, a step too far. I'd almost finished my coffee when a woman crept under my table, to hide from her partner. That was my cue to drink up and leave.

I was halfway up the high street when I spotted Betty Longbottom walking towards me. Her hair was looking much better than it had the last time we'd spoken—the new style suited her. What I didn't understand is why she had her hand over her right eye.

"Hi, Betty, I like what you've done with your hair."

"Thanks, Jill."

"Are you okay? Do you have something in your eye?"

"Err, no. I'm fine, thanks."

"Are you sure? Let me take a look. Maybe I can—" And then I saw it. "Oh?"

She must have realised that I'd seen her missing eyebrow because she lowered her hand. "What am I supposed to do now, Jill?"

"When did that happen?"

"Just now. I've just this minute come out of Nailed-It."

Oh bum! I'd been the one who'd suggested that Betty go to Deli's salon for eyebrow threading. With a bit of luck she would have forgotten that.

"I wish you'd never told me about that stupid salon, Jill."

"I'm sorry. I—err—"

"That ridiculous man obviously doesn't have a clue

what he's doing. I was lucky to get out of there with one eyebrow still intact."

"Man?"

"Yeah. I thought it was unusual for a man to be doing it, but I figured he must be qualified, or they wouldn't let him near the customers. Clearly, I was wrong."

"What are you going to do?"

"Sue their sorry backsides."

"I meant about — err — that?"

"I don't know; it'll take weeks to grow back. I'll just have to pencil it in until then, I suppose." She put her hand back over her eye. "I'd better get going."

"Okay. Sorry again."

Deli had told me she'd employed a specialist to provide the eyebrow threading service. What was her name? Fifi Lasso or something. So, who was the man who had made such a mess of Betty's eyebrow? Surely not Nails?

***

I'd promised to contact the two applicants for the post of office manager today, to let them know if they'd been successful or not. Unfortunately, I was no closer to deciding between the two Robinson brothers. Somehow, though, I would have to make my decision before close of business today.

"I wish you'd left that stupid cat at your house," Mrs V said.

"What's he done?"

"I thought I'd check he was still okay, and he hissed at me. I thought he was going to go for me."

"Maybe you just startled him?"

"He deliberately ambushed me. He saw me come into the room, and never stirred, but as soon as I got close to him, his fur stood on end and he hissed like something possessed."

"It's probably the after-effects of whatever was ailing him yesterday. I'm sure it won't happen again."

"Hey, Winky! I want a word."

"Moi?" He gave me that butter-wouldn't-melt look of his.

"What are you playing at?"

"I'm just sitting here, minding my own business."

"You attacked Mrs V."

"Don't be ridiculous. I just scared her a little."

"Why would you do that?"

"She was beginning to get the wrong idea about our relationship. She thought we were BFFs, so I had to nip that in the bud pretty sharpish."

"Why can't you just be nice to her like you were this morning?"

"I was still delirious at the joy of getting away from Snowball. I didn't know what I was doing."

"Just don't hiss at her again, or you'll have me to answer to."

"Whatever."

I took a coin out of my pocket and handed it to him.

"What's this for?"

"I want you to toss it."

"Why?"

"Just do it."

"Okay." He flipped the coin, and then caught it on top of his paw. "It's tails."

"Thanks."

"What was that all about?" He looked more than a little puzzled.

"Nothing you need trouble your head with."

Little did he know, but he'd just helped me to choose my new office manager. Alistair Robinson it was.

What? I only said that *I* wouldn't toss a coin to make such an important decision. I didn't say anything about not getting my cat to do it for me.

***

I'd managed to contact both of Royston Rhodes' ex-partners, and once I'd told them what had happened to Daze, they'd been more than willing to talk to me. She was obviously well regarded in the rogue retriever community—something that couldn't be said for Rhodes. To save time, they'd agreed to speak to me together.

As both of them were still based in London, it made sense for us to meet there, so I magicked myself to Charing Cross station, and met them in a small coffee shop on the Strand.

They were easy to pick out even though neither of them was wearing the trademark catsuit. Both men were at least six-six and built like brick—you get the picture.

"Hi, I'm Jill. Thanks for taking time to speak to me."

"No problem." The blond was the first to shake my hand. "I'm Graham Marshall, but everyone calls me Radar."

"And I'm Charlie Brent." The second guy had a shaven head. "Better known as Bazaar."

"One thing I'm curious about," Radar said. "How did

you manage to get our names?"

"Let's just say that Daze has a lot of friends inside the department. I'd rather not name names, though."

"Fair enough. I couldn't believe it when I heard she was under investigation. They don't come any better than Daze. Rhodes can't hold a candle to her."

"You're not a fan of his, I take it?"

"The man's a liability. He's the closest thing to useless I've ever seen, and I've had a lot of partners over the years."

"It was the same when he worked with me," Bazaar said. "The man was clueless. I was quite relieved when he went lone wolf on me."

"How did that come about?"

"Going lone wolf? He just started to go missing. If it had been anyone else, I'd have called them out on it, but to be perfectly honest, it was easier to work by myself."

"Same thing happened with me." Radar nodded. "After the first couple of weeks, I barely saw the man."

"The thing I don't understand is, if he's so useless, how come he has the highest arrest rate of any rogue retriever in the country? It isn't even a close contest. He has twice as many as anyone else."

The two men both shrugged.

"It makes no sense to me," Radar said. "I wouldn't have believed that the man I knew would have been capable of making a single arrest."

"That's what I've been trying to work out too," Bazaar said. "I just don't get it."

"I'll be perfectly honest with you both. The main reason I wanted to meet with you was in the hope that you might have some dirt on Rhodes. Something I could use as leverage to get him to drop the inquiry into Daze."

"I really wish I had something for you," Radar said. "I've been racking my brain for something. Anything. But the man is squeaky clean. Totally useless, but squeaky clean."

"Likewise," Bazaar chipped in. "I don't have any dirt on him either." He hesitated. "There is one thing I find a little peculiar, but I don't see how it's going to help you."

"Tell me. Anything's better than what I have right now, which is zip."

"Okay. I've seen his record, and all his arrests are witches who had been married to humans."

"You mean witches who let it slip to their husbands that they were sups?"

"Yeah. Every rogue retriever I know has a mix of collars: Witches, wizards, vampires, werewolves and the rest. But not Rhodes. They're all witches and they were all arrested for the same offence."

"That is weird. Could you possibly let me have contact details for a couple of the humans whose wives were taken back to Candlefield?"

"What good would that do?"

"Maybe none, but right now, it's the only lead I have."

After we'd finished, Radar and Bazaar went on their way. I hung back because I wanted to call the two candidates for the post of office manager. Craig was understandably disappointed not to have got the job, but he accepted my decision with good grace.

"Is that Alistair?"

"Speaking."

"Alistair, it's Jill Maxwell. I promised I'd call you by the end of the week about the office manager job."

"Right?"

"I'm very pleased to confirm that your application has been successful, and I'd like to offer you the post at the salary we discussed."

"That's fantastic. Thank you so much."

"There's just the question of when you can start?"

"I'm only on one week's notice, so if I hand my resignation in now, I can join you a week on Monday."

"That sounds great. I'll look forward to seeing you then."

***

I called in at the Corner Shop on my way home. As usual, Little Jack was on his wooden box behind the counter. He didn't see me come in because he was too busy polishing the trophies he'd won in the recent stacking competition.

"You'll wear those out," I said.

"Sorry, Jill. I didn't see you there. Custard creams is it?"

"Actually, I need a few things today." I took out the short list that I'd scribbled earlier.

"In that case, maybe you'd like to avail yourself of our new service?"

"What's that?"

"We're now offering home delivery."

"What does that cost?"

"Nothing. It's a free service to anyone who spends more than ten pounds. Looking at the items on your list, I can see that you qualify."

"How can you afford to do that?"

"It's a case of having to. We have to compete with the big boys who are all offering a delivery service these days."

"But don't they charge for it?"

"They do. That's our competitive advantage. We only offer it to those who live in a two-mile radius, though."

"In that case, I'll definitely take you up on it." I hesitated. "Just one thing: When would it be delivered? I'm going to need some of the items on this list to make dinner tonight."

"Fret not. Everything will be with you within forty-minutes."

"Excellent."

"You haven't heard the best part yet, Jill."

"Oh?"

"In a few days' time, I'll be launching an app that will allow you to place your order from the comfort of your home."

"Wow! I'm very impressed."

You had to hand it to Little Jack, he was always looking for new ways to improve his business. A little like me, really.

Britt must have seen me pull onto the drive because she came rushing out of the house, and called me over.

"I'm sorry to trouble you, err—"

"Jill."

"Right. Lovely has been driving me crazy all day. She's usually very quiet, but she keeps jumping onto the fence and meowing at your house. I think she's missing your cat. Do you fasten him indoors when you go to work?"

"I don't actually have a cat."

"But I saw you bring him home in a basket yesterday; he and Lovely were together last night. She seems quite smitten by him."

"Oh, that cat. He isn't mine. I was just looking after him for a friend. He's back home now."

"Oh dear. How very disappointing. Lovely will be devastated."

"There are plenty more cats in the sea. I'm sure she'll make other friends."

"I do hope so. The move hasn't been easy for her." Britt started back to the door, but then hesitated. "Am I going crazy or has that sprouted up overnight?" She pointed to the tree in Tony and Clare's front garden.

"I'm pretty sure it's always been there."

She laughed. "I must be even less observant than I thought I was."

On my way into the house, I said to the tree, "It's okay, Mr Hosey, your secret is safe with me."

"Thanks, Jill."

***

I was in the lounge when Jack came storming into the house. He was red-faced, and clearly annoyed about something.

"Whatever is the matter?"

"Shouldn't be allowed on the road!"

"Who shouldn't?"

"I'd just turned onto our estate when a young woman on a bike came sailing across the road in front of me. She obviously had no idea how to ride it. I only just managed to swerve in time, otherwise she would have been a goner."

"Take a deep breath. It's okay now."

"That's her!" He pointed out of the window. "Just look at her! She's all over the place." He was right; the young woman was going from one side of the road to the other. It didn't help that the basket on the front of the bike was clearly overloaded. "She's pulled onto our drive."

Only then did I realise who the young woman was: Lucy Locket.

Jack followed me to the door.

"Your delivery, Jill." She handed me the basket of groceries.

"Are you sure this is safe, Lucy?" I said. "You looked like you were struggling just now."

"I was. I've never ridden a bike in my life before this week. When Little Jack came up with this latest brainwave of his, he didn't think to check if I could ride a bike."

Chapter 12

"I wouldn't want you to feel bad about leaving me all alone this weekend." I was still in bed. Jack was busy packing his overnight bag.

"It's okay. I don't. I've asked you to come with me a dozen times, but you turned me down."

"I'll be all alone here in this empty house. With nothing to do."

"If you're trying to guilt-trip me, it isn't going to work. It's your own fault that you're staying behind."

"Of course, if someone was to make me a full English breakfast before that someone left me all alone for the weekend, then maybe I wouldn't feel quite so bad about it."

"Fine, I'll make you breakfast, but only because I want one too."

"Did I ever tell you that you're my favourite husband?"

"Forget the soft-soap. It doesn't wash. By the way, I meant to ask you last night, did you decide who to give the office manager job to?"

"Yeah. Alistair Robinson will be joining me a week on Monday."

"How did you decide between them in the end?"

"It wasn't easy. I had to employ advanced HR analysis techniques."

"You tossed a coin, didn't you?"

"Certainly not."

"You definitely tossed a coin."

"On my life, I promise. *I* didn't toss a coin."

Good as his word, Jack had a full English breakfast

waiting for me when I came downstairs.

"That looks delicious." I gave him a kiss. "I forgive you for abandoning me."

"What will you do all weekend?"

"Actually, I might work. There's a couple of people I'd like to talk to if I can get hold of them."

"In connection with that missing woman?"

"One of them, yeah. The other is related to the Daze problem I told you about."

"How's that going? Are we in the clear yet?"

"Not while she's still under investigation. I'm trying to get an angle on this new boss of hers; there's something about him that doesn't ring true. Oh, and I've also got to go to Candlefield for the baby competition. That should be a good laugh."

"You're really horrible to your cousins."

"How am *I* the horrible one? It's their own fault for keeping secrets from one another. I just hope neither Lil nor Lily wins because if they do, things are going to get ugly. Oh yes, I almost forgot. I also have to try and get Rhymes' poetry published. The problem is I don't have a clue where to start."

"I might be able to help with that."

"What do you know about tortoise poetry?"

"Very little, but one of the guys at our station recently got his book published. Something about steam engines I think. I could ask him how he went about it if you like?"

"That would be great." I blew him a kiss. "You're the best."

"What about the author's name? I can hardly list it as Rhymes the tortoise, can I?"

"I guess not. How about Robert Hymes? That would

make him R. Hymes."

***

One of Jack's bowling buddies picked him up from outside our house. All four of them in the car looked so excited.

Tragic really.

I'd managed to contact Pam Turton's friend, Carly Broome, and she'd agreed to see me this morning. In the afternoon, I was hoping to grab a word with one of the men whose wife had been sent back to Candlefield by Royston Rhodes.

"Hiya!" Britt called to me as I was about to get into the car.

"Hi." I really wasn't in the mood for another sob story about how much her cat was missing Winky.

"It's moved."

"Moved? What's moved?"

"You remember yesterday, I said that I didn't remember seeing that tree in your other neighbour's garden?"

"Err, kind of."

"Well, it's gone again. Look!" She pointed to Tony and Clare's front garden, which was now minus Mr Hosey's tree.

"Wow, you're right. Maybe the wind blew it down? There was quite a gale last night."

"Was there? I didn't hear anything."

"Yes, it was very strong."

"But there's no sign of the tree at all."

"Strange that. Anyway, I must get going. I have to work

today."

"Of course. I'm sorry to have delayed you."

Just then, I spotted a bush moving in the garden across the road. Thankfully, Britt didn't.

***

Carly Broome lived in a small flat overlooking the canal. In her mid-twenties, she clearly had a thing about kangaroos: The door knocker was a kangaroo, the curtains had a kangaroo motif, and she answered the door wearing a woolly sweater with a kangaroo on the front.

"Carly? I'm Jill Maxwell."

"Come in. I only have about thirty minutes because I've got a meeting of the WWAS this morning."

"WWAS?"

"The Washbridge Wallaby Appreciation Society. We meet on the first Saturday of every month."

"I thought those were kangaroos?"

"What?" She looked mortified. "How could you possibly confuse the two?"

"Sorry. I'm not particularly well versed on marsupials."

"Clearly not."

Although we hadn't got off to the best of starts, marsupially speaking, Carly proved to be very pleasant and eager to help.

"From what I know of Pam," I said. "She doesn't appear to have many friends?"

"You're right. She can be a little awkward around people at times, but she and I seemed to hit it off from the get-go. Do you think she's okay?"

"That's what I'm hoping to find out. When exactly did

you last see her?"

"It must have been about three weeks ago because I remember telling her about our last WWAS meeting."

"Was she interested in Wallabies too?"

"Not really, but she's a good listener. That's one of the things I like about Pam."

"Where did you meet?"

"We both worked at the same bar for a while: Liberty's, do you know it?"

"Yes, I went there on my sister's birthday a couple of years ago."

I'd tried to erase the memory of that day from my mind. Like an idiot, I'd spent all day magicking myself back and forth between Kathy's birthday party and my mother's wedding.

"I didn't last very long at Liberty's," Carly said. "They objected to me wearing my wallaby tights."

"What about Pam?"

"She still works there."

"How was she the last time you saw her?"

"Fine. In fact, she was much happier than I'd seen her for a while."

"Any particular reason?"

"Probably because of Duncan."

"Who's that?"

"I don't know his surname. He works with her at Liberty's; he started there after I'd left."

"Was she seeing him?"

"She said not, but the way she spoke about him, I got the feeling there was something going on."

"Pam's sister didn't mention him."

"Like I said, Pam didn't actually say they were an item,

so maybe there was nothing to tell."

"Did you know that Pam had run away several times as a teenager?" I asked.

"Yes, she told me all about it."

"Do you think she might have done it again?"

"No. Definitely not. She loves that boat. Have you seen it?"

"I have. She's made a good job of it."

"She put her heart and soul into renovating it. I can't believe she'd just up and leave."

"What do you think has happened to her, then?"

"I honestly don't know. Nothing bad I hope."

***

I magicked myself over to Candlefield Community Centre where Aunt Lucy was waiting for me. On her left, was Pearl who was rocking Lily in her arms. On her right, were Amber and Lil. The twins were both red in the face and doing their best not to look at one another. I suspected the reason Aunt Lucy was standing in between them was to keep the peace.

"Hello, Aunt Lucy. Hello you two."

"You knew about this, didn't you, Jill?" Pearl snapped.

"Why didn't you say something?" Amber said.

"Don't take it out on me. You're the ones who are behaving like children. You should have told one another about the competition."

"I explained why I didn't want to say anything," Pearl said. "I didn't want Amber to feel bad when Lily wins."

"That's a joke!" Amber shot back. "You're the one who's going to be upset when Lil takes home the trophy. That's why I didn't tell you. I didn't want to hurt your feelings."

"In your dreams is Lil ever going to beat Lily."

"It's obvious to anyone that Lil is prettier than Lily."

"That's enough!" Aunt Lucy shouted. "You're sisters. You're supposed to be supportive of one another."

"I'm trying to be, Mum," Amber said. "But it's obvious to anyone that—"

"I don't want to hear any more about it. The judges will make their own minds up. Speaking of which, if we don't get inside soon, both babies will be disqualified for being late."

The twins were still exchanging barbed comments on their way inside.

The hall where the competition was taking place was packed with parents and their tiny offspring.

"Why aren't Alan and William here today?" I asked.

"Alan has to work," Pearl said.

"William too, but he's going to make room for the trophy when he gets home."

"That'll be a waste of his time." Pearl scoffed.

Aunt Lucy was just about to let rip at the twins again when a woman, wearing a hat that looked very much like a dead rat, took to the stage.

"What has she got on her head?" I whispered to Aunt Lucy.

"I've no idea, but it looks awful."

"Mums, dads, grandparents and babies, welcome to the annual Candlefield Beautiful Baby Competition. It's good to see so many of you here today. As you know, the parents of the competitors submitted photographs of their little darlings earlier this week. The judges have spent the last two days going through those photographs in order to select the final ten. I have here the list of the ten babies selected to go through to the final. If I call your baby's name, please go through the door to my left where the judges will pick the three winners."

"You'll stay and watch if Lily doesn't get called, won't you?" Amber said to Pearl.

"Like that's going to happen."

"Okay, here goes." The woman adjusted her hat, which now appeared to be trying to chew the top of her ear. "In no particular order, here are your ten finalists."

The four of us hung on her every word as she called out the names. With nine babies already sent through to the next room, neither Lil nor Lily's name had been called out.

"It has to be Lil next," Amber said.

"No chance. It's bound to be Lily."

"And the tenth and last baby to make it into the final is Li—" Both of the twins stepped forward. "Linda Trustmore." That stopped them dead in their tracks. The expression on their faces was a mix of disbelief and disgust.

"How could they not pick Lily or Lil?" Pearl said.

"Those judges clearly don't know what they're doing." Amber huffed. "We're leaving."

"Wait for me," Pearl called after her. "We'll come with you."

When Aunt Lucy turned to me, she had a huge grin on her face. "Now that's what I call a result."

***

I was becoming a regular visitor to London.

Bazaar had given me the names of two men whose wives had been taken back to Candlefield by Royston Rhodes. The first of those was Joe Garland whose wife, Suzy, had disappeared just over nine months ago.

"Thanks for agreeing to see me, Mr Garland."

"It's Joe. I was surprised to get your call, particularly when you said you were a witch married to a human too. There aren't many people — well no one really — that I can talk to about this."

"How long had you known that your wife was a witch before she was taken away?"

"Only a matter of days."

"And how long had you been together by then?"

"We met over two years ago, and we hit it off straight away."

"And you didn't have a clue that she was a witch until just before she was snatched?"

"None."

"What made her decide to let you in on her secret?"

"She didn't. That's the frustrating part. Suzy never breathed a word about being a witch to me."

"So how did you find out?"

"Someone sent a video to me by email."

"What was on it?"

"Suzy, performing all kinds of magic spells. I thought it was some kind of prank at first, but when I showed it to her, she broke down and told me everything. I was shocked of course, but it didn't make any difference to how I felt about her."

"Did she warn you not to tell anyone else?"

"Of course, and I didn't. Why would I? She'd told me what would happen if those retrievers found out. I wasn't going to risk losing her."

"But they found out anyway. Could Suzy have told anyone else that you knew her secret?"

"No, definitely not. She was just as scared of what would happen as I was."

"So how did the rogue retrievers find out?"

"I have no idea."

"What about the email address that the video came from?"

"I sent a few messages to it, but they all just bounced back. Whoever did it must have been using a temporary account."

"Did your wife have any idea how the video came into existence?"

"Yeah. She reckoned it must have been taken at the dating agency."

"Dating agency?"

"Sorry, I should have said. That's how we met."

"Why would they have taken a video of her performing spells?"

"Suzy said they insisted she perform a number of spells to prove she was a witch."

"They should have been able to tell that just by looking at her."

"That's what she said, but anyway she did it. She had no idea that they were videoing her at the time."

"What was the name of the dating agency? Do you remember?"

"Yeah. The Crystal Dating Agency; they have a small office on Carnaby Street."

Something was definitely off. Why would a dating

agency surreptitiously video their clients performing magic, and then use those videos to 'out' them? There was only one reason I could think of, but before I jumped to conclusions, I wanted to speak to Andy Poulter, the second name on Bazaar's list. He was unavailable this weekend, so I'd arranged to see him on Monday. I had a feeling his story might be very similar, and if so, my next port of call would be the Crystal Dating Agency.

Chapter 13

I'd spent all of Sunday tidying the garden, cleaning the car and sorting out the spare bedroom.

Oh, wait a minute. Those were the things I'd thought about doing. What I actually did was binge out on boxsets and order in pizza.

What? Don't judge. I needed to recharge my batteries ahead of a busy week.

Needless to say, when Jack had got back, he was full of the ten-pin bowling tournament, and had been kind enough to talk me through it frame by frame.

"I didn't tell you what happened in the final," he said, the next morning over breakfast.

"Are you sure? I feel as though you talked me through every frame played since the game was invented."

"I started to tell you about it, but you'd fallen asleep by the time I got to the third frame."

"Right. Unfortunately, I have to rush out this morning, so you'll have to save it for later."

"Okay. When? Tonight?"

"Maybe." I gave him a kiss. "Take care. See you later."

I loved every square inch of that guy, but if I had to listen to him talk about splits, washouts or turkeys for one more minute, I'd be forced to kill him. What were turkeys doing in a bowling alley anyway?

"Morning, Jill!" Tony called from next door. He and Clare were just on their way out.

"Morning. Have you come up with a theme for your con yet?" I did my best to feign interest.

"Not yet." Clare frowned. "I don't suppose you've had any more bright ideas for us, have you?"

"How about TenPinCon?" I joked.

The two of them exchanged a glance, and their faces lit up.

"You're a genius, Jill," Tony said.

"That's a brilliant idea," Clare gushed.

"I wasn't actually being—"

"Isn't Jack into ten-pin bowling?" Tony was really fired up now.

"Oh yes, he most certainly is."

"Do you think he might be willing to act as consultant for the con if we went ahead with it?"

"Are you kidding? He'd kill to be involved. He's in the house now; why don't you go and have a word with him? If you ask him nicely, he'll probably tell you all about the tournament he went to this weekend."

The two of them practically trampled me underfoot as they rushed by.

***

As I walked from the car towards my office building, I was still half-asleep. That soon changed when I saw the scene outside.

Half a dozen clowns were gathered around the doorway, doing their stuff. Only then did I remember that Clown was opening its doors to its first 'students' today. As I got closer, I realised that one of the clowns was Sneezy.

"Morning, Snee—" I didn't quite manage to get the words out before a jet of water, from the flower on his lapel, hit me in the face.

"Morning, Jill. It's our big day today."

"So I see." I wiped the water from my eye.

"There are still a couple of places in the first class if you'd like to sign up?"

"Tempting as that is, I've got a busy week ahead of me." I glanced around at the other clowns. "Are these some of your students?"

"Goodness me, no. These guys are all seasoned performers. That's Chuckles."

Chuckles offered his hand, but I wasn't falling for that one again. I just nodded at him.

"Then we have Bingo, Noodles, and Giggles. They'll all be working as instructors in the school."

"It's a pleasure to meet you all," I lied, then I began to edge my way past them into the building. "I hope it all goes okay today."

Having to run the gauntlet of a bunch of clowns every morning wasn't my idea of fun. It's not that I'm afraid of them, despite what Kathy would have you believe, I simply don't find them funny.

Still, at least my offices were a clown-free zone.

Spoke too soon.

What the—? I stopped dead in my tracks when I saw the clown sitting at Mrs V's desk.

"What are you doing in here? You should be next door!"

"It's only me, dear," the clown said in Mrs V's voice. "What do you think of my outfit?"

I was too stunned to speak; the only sound that came from my mouth was a series of grunts.

Mrs V, or whatever that 'thing' was, continued, "I've decided to call myself Knittie. What do you think?"

"I—err—"

"Since Armi was demoted by the Cuckoo Clock Appreciation Society, he's been looking for a new hobby. I just happened to mention the clown school, and he suggested we should both sign up for it."

"Armi? I can't believe he wants to do that."

"I haven't seen him so excited about anything in a long time. He's chosen Jingles as his clown name. Don't worry, dear, we've signed up for the evening classes, so I won't need to take time off work."

"Right."

"I wanted you to see my costume. Be honest, what do you think? Is the red nose too big?"

"It's—err, I think I heard my phone. I'd better go and answer it."

At least the clowns couldn't get to me in my office.

What the—?

Sitting on my desk was a Winky shaped clown.

"What do you think?" He chuckled. "I'm going to call myself Furball."

"Get off my desk and take off that ridiculous costume."

"What's wrong? You aren't scared of a little clown, are you?"

"Of course I'm not scared, but this office is a clown no-go area."

"I kind of like the feel of this costume."

"If you don't take it off in the next five minutes, I'll take you home with me, and you can live with Lovely."

I'd never seen anyone shed a costume so quickly.

"Satisfied?" He huffed.

"Thank you."

"You should go next door and sign up for one of their classes." Winky jumped onto the sofa.

"Why would I want to do that?"

"Because you're such a misery guts these days. Being a clown might cheer you up a bit."

"I'm not miserable. I'm a laugh a minute."

"Not according to the laughometer. And besides, it would help you to get rid of all that stress you carry around."

"I'm not stressed either."

"You're a tightly coiled spring that could explode at any moment."

"You need to unmix your metaphors. Since when did a spring explode?"

"See, you've just proven my point: you have zero sense of humour."

***

When I left the office thirty minutes later, Mrs V, AKA Knittie, was busy knitting.

"I've got quite a few people to see today, err—Mrs V. I'm not sure what time I'll be back, if at all."

"Alright dear." Her little hat rose slowly off her head. "I'll call you if anything urgent crops up."

"Were you thinking of keeping that outfit on all day?"

"I thought I might. I need to wear it in."

"Right."

I tried not to think about what kind of first impression that would give to any would-be clients who came to the office.

Andy Poulter, the second name on Bazaar's list, worked
nightshifts as a porter at his local hospital. He'd agreed to
speak to me this morning when he got back from his shift,
before he went to bed.

The poor man looked dead on his feet.

"Come in." He yawned. "Sorry, I've had a tiring night."

"I really appreciate you sparing the time to speak to me.
I promise I won't keep you long. You must be ready for
your bed."

"That's okay, but you'll have to excuse me if I yawn. I
was surprised when you said you were a witch too. And
your husband is a human, is that right?"

"Yes."

"Aren't you putting yourself in danger by doing this?
Look what happened to Kathleen."

"Is that your wife?"

He nodded. "I miss her something terrible. Do you
think there's any chance you might be able to get her
back?"

"I'm really sorry, but I don't think that's very likely. I
am hoping you can help me to stop this happening to
anyone else, though."

"If I can, I will."

"How long had you been together before Kathleen told
you she was a witch?"

"She didn't tell me, that's what really irks. I would
never have known if it hadn't been for that video."

I'd half-expected him to say that.

"What was on it?"

"It was Kathleen, performing a number of different

magic spells. When I showed it to her, she broke down and told me everything. Then she made me promise I'd never tell anyone her secret, and I haven't, but a few days later, they took her away."

"Do you know who sent you the video?"

"Kathleen reckoned it must have been made while she was at the dating agency."

"Would that have been the Crystal Dating Agency by any chance?"

"Yes, how did you know?"

"Because you aren't the only couple this has happened to."

"Why would a dating agency do something like this?"

"I'm not sure, but I intend to find out."

***

I'd promised Butter that I would meet with her plantation manager, Thistle Patch, in an attempt to try and find out why they were experiencing water shortages in all of their plantations.

"Call me Patch." The jolly fairy greeted me with a smile and a firm handshake. "The queen told me you'd be coming over today. I'm sorry I wasn't around last week to see you."

"That's okay. Maybe we could start with you showing me around?"

"My pleasure. This is the original plantation, which was hit badly this year. Judging by what her majesty told me, you'll already be aware of that."

"Yes, that's how I first came to be involved. Things seem to be much better at the moment." I looked out over field after field of beautiful flowers.

"It might seem that way, but the water supply is running dangerously low. Come and see for yourself." He led the way along the path that ran around the fields of flowers. Look over there."

The small reservoir was almost dry.

"How long will that last?" I said.

"Not long enough. I don't understand it. There's been plenty of rain on the high ground, and there are no blockages in the streams leading down to the reservoir. By rights, this reservoir should be almost full."

"Butter, err—I mean, the queen mentioned that it was the same at the other plantations too."

"That's right, which is even more perplexing. I chose them because of their excellent water supply. Would you like to see the others?"

"Maybe just one other. I don't think I need to see them all. Shall I magic us over there?"

"I'd rather you didn't." Patch took a step back. "I don't really like all that magic stuff."

"But aren't you a fairy?"

"Yes, but we floral fairies gave up magic many years ago; we just focus on the flowers these days."

"It won't hurt. I promise."

"I'd rather take Peg if you don't mind."

"*Peg?*"

"Here girl!" he shouted.

I followed his gaze skywards, and moments later, a winged horse appeared through the clouds.

"You don't expect me to ride on that thing, do you?"

"I heard on the grapevine that you'd ridden on a dragon's back in the Elite Competition."

"Yes, but that was—"

"You have nothing to worry about with Peg, does she, girl?" He stroked the horse's mane. "Hop on." He gave me a hand up, and then climbed on behind me. "Let's go, girl. Take us to the west plantation."

To be fair, the ride was very smooth, and not nearly as scary as the journey when Sybil had been rushing back to check on Cora. In no time at all, we were descending again.

"That wasn't too bad, was it?" Patch said, once we'd both dismounted.

"No, it was fine. Thanks, Peg."

The horse nodded her goodbyes, and then flew off towards the clouds.

"Look!" Patch pointed to the reservoir where the water levels were even lower. "When I was scouting regions for the new plantations, one of the main criteria was an abundant water supply. This particular region was the best of the bunch. If anything, I was a little concerned there might be too much rainfall, but look at the water level."

"Has there been less rainfall than you expected?"

"No, that's just it. If anything, there's been more. It doesn't make sense."

"What do you think is happening, Patch?"

"The queen asked me the same question before she called you in. The only thing that makes any sense is sabotage. I think someone is deliberately trying to wreck our operation."

"Who would do that?"

"I honestly don't know. I just concentrate on growing the flowers. I don't get involved with the commercial side of the business. You'd need to speak to the queen about that."

"Would it be possible to let me know if things get any worse?"

"Of course. The easiest way would probably be to add your phone number to the auto-alarm—that sends a text to me if the levels become dangerously low."

"That sounds like a plan."

Chapter 14

Even though the journey aboard the winged horse hadn't been half as bad as I'd expected, I still chose to magic myself over to Hyacinth House. I didn't have an appointment to see Butter, but once reception called to say I was there, she had me sent to her office straight away.

"I've just been with Patch," I said.

"Did he show you the water levels?"

"Yes. I only saw two of the plantations, but I understand from him that the others are the same."

"What did you make of it?"

"It's pretty obvious something is amiss. Patch reckons the rainfall in all of the regions is as expected or better, and he's checked all the feeder streams, but found no blockages. He seems to think this could be sabotage."

"It's hard for me to believe that anyone would stoop so low as to do something like this."

"Can you think of another explanation for what's happening?"

"No." She shook her head.

"I asked Patch if he had any idea who might be behind it, but he said I should speak to you about that. Who would benefit most from damaging your business?"

"We only really have two serious competitors: Pixie Petals and Always Flowers."

"What can you tell me about them?"

"I honestly don't believe that Pixie Petals would do something like this. They've been in business for almost as long as we have. Although we're competitors, we have a great deal of respect for one another. We've helped them out when they've been in trouble and vice versa."

"What about Always Flowers?"

"They're much newer, and their business model is quite different to ours and Pixie Petals."

"How so?"

"The floral fairies and Pixie Petals grow and sell flowers. Always Flowers manufacture them."

"Are you talking about artificial flowers?"

"Yes. Don't get me wrong, they're made to a very high standard, and from a distance, they might pass as the real thing. Fortunately for us, most people still seem to prefer real flowers."

"What kind of relationship do you have with them?"

"Always Flowers? Not so good. My mother had a few run-ins with them in recent years. Fortunately, that isn't something I've had to contend with so far."

"Unless of course they're behind this?"

"True, but I find it really hard to believe they'd do something like this. Previously, our issues with them have related to over aggressive marketing on their part. They once had their people standing outside all of the florists in Candlefield, giving out free samples. My mother went ballistic when she found out. But the thing is, it was just marketing. Aggressive perhaps, but certainly nothing illegal."

"Nevertheless, I think I should talk to someone there, and at Pixie Petals. Can you let me know who would be the best people to speak to?"

"Of course."

At that moment, the doors to Butter's office flew open, and in stormed a young fairy. "How dare you, Butter?"

"Tulip, this isn't the time." Butter gestured towards me. "I have a visitor."

"Stuff your visitor! How dare you cut my allowance again without so much as a word?"

"I told you last week that there would have to be more cuts all around because of the crop failure."

"You didn't say you'd be cutting *my* money again. You'd already cut it by a quarter."

"You aren't the only one to have their allowance reduced. All members of the royal family have had to accept similar additional reductions."

"Not you, though, I don't suppose?"

"Of course I have."

"I don't believe you! I'm not going to stand for this. You'll see."

"We'll talk later, Tulip. After my guest has left."

"There's nothing to talk about." And with that, she stormed out of the room.

"I apologise for the interruption, Jill." Butter looked mortified by the outburst. "That was Tulip, my younger sister. What were we talking about before she came in?"

"I was asking if you'd let me have contact details for the people I should speak to at Pixie Petals and Always Flowers."

"Of course. I'll have Heather provide you with them."

I could sympathise with Butter. I knew what it was like to be the reasonable sister, and have to put up with the rantings of a sibling.

***

Suki Coates was the other person whose boat had been burgled recently. As I didn't have a phone number for her,

I arrived at her boat on spec, in the hope that she'd be home and would be willing to speak to me.

I managed to board the boat without falling in the drink, which was a promising start. No one answered on my first knock. Or the second. After the third, I was just about to give up when the door swung open.

The bleary-eyed woman was dressed in red PJs.

"What do you want?"

"Sorry. Did I wake you?"

"Didn't you see the name of the boat?"

"Err, yeah?"

"I don't do mornings. When I retired, I promised myself I'd never see another morning. I usually get up around midday."

"Sorry. I didn't make the connection."

"Who are you, anyway? What do you want? If you're selling something, you're out of luck. I'm broke."

"I'm not selling anything. My name is Jill Maxwell; I'm a private investigator. I'm looking into the disappearance of a woman who lives on a boat on this canal: Pam Turton."

"I know Pam." She rubbed the sleep from her eyes. "The Green Lady, right?"

"That's right."

"What do you mean by *disappeared*?"

"Just that. Her sister came to see me because Pam has gone missing."

"You'd better come below."

"Thanks." I followed her down the steps. "This is beautiful."

"It's only small, but I like it. I'd better make some coffee, or I'll fall asleep on you. Would you like one?"

"Yes, please."

Once we had our drinks, we sat at the small table at the far end of the living area.

"I spoke to the Trumans last week. They told me you'd been to France."

"Tommy and Doris? Such a lovely couple. Yes, I went to stay with an old school friend who has retired out there. Cheap holidays are the only kind I can afford now."

"You know Pam, then?"

"Not well. She's just a youngster; she and I don't really have much in common. When we have spoken, it's been about her boat. She's done a super job, considering the state of it when she moved in. Do you have any clues where she might have gone?"

"None so far. One lead I'm following up is the recent burglaries."

"I see. I wondered why you wanted to speak to me. You heard I was burgled, I take it?"

"Yes, the people at the Canal Authority gave me the Trumans' name and yours. Could you tell me what happened?"

"There's not much to tell. I was luckier than the Trumans, I suppose."

"How do you mean?"

"I came home and disturbed the punk before he could take anything."

"That could have been nasty."

"I suppose so, but it all happened so quickly that I didn't get the chance to think about the danger. He saw me and made a dash for it."

"Did you get a good look at him?"

"No, the boat was in darkness. He pushed past me and

made a run for it—empty-handed, thank goodness."

"And you can't describe him at all?"

"Not really, but I reckon he'll have a cut on his face."

"How do you know that if you couldn't see him?"

"I lashed out at him as he pushed by me, and I caught him in the face." She took out her phone and brought up a photo of a small stud. "I reckon that will have left a mark when it was ripped out."

"Where's the stud now?"

"The police took it as evidence. I told them everything I've just told you, but I haven't heard anything since. It's the Trumans I feel sorry for. Did you know they're thinking of giving up High Kicker?"

"Yeah, they told me."

"Such a shame. They love that boat, but the break-in seems to have rattled them."

"Did you ever see Pam with anyone else?"

"I didn't see her very often at all to be honest. There was one occasion when I saw her walking down the towpath with a young fellow. At least, I think she was with him."

"You aren't sure?"

"They weren't walking side by side like you'd expect a young couple to do. He was a few feet behind her, as though they'd fallen out and weren't speaking to one another."

"When was this?"

"I don't remember exactly—a few weeks ago maybe."

"Can you describe him?"

"I didn't get a good look at him. Curly hair, though; I do remember that."

"Have you seen her since then?"

"Yes, I saw her a few days afterwards. She seemed fine

then."

***

Carly Broome had mentioned that Pam Turton worked in Liberty's bar, and that she'd been seeing one of the guys who worked alongside her. Despite the bad memories that particular establishment held for me, I decided to pay it a visit to see if I could grab a word with Duncan.

The bar was almost unrecognisable since my last visit. About the only thing that hadn't changed was the name. When I arrived there, the place was heaving, and it took me some time to fight my way to the bar.

"What can I get for you?" The young woman's name tag read: Kirsty.

"I'm looking for Duncan. Is he working today?"

"Duncan?" She pulled a face like she'd just bitten on a lemon. "He isn't here."

"Do you know when he's due in next?"

"He's off ill, I think. Sorry."

"Could you ask him to give me a call when he gets back?"

"I suppose so."

I handed her my card, which she stuffed into her pocket, before moving on to serve the next customer.

***

When I got back to the office building, there were not one, but two clowns in the outer office.

"What do you think of Jingles?" Knittie said.

"Armi?"

"Hi, Jill."

If it hadn't been for his voice, I would never have known it was him underneath all the makeup and the ridiculous costume.

"This is a surprise." And not a pleasant one.

"Our first class is this evening," Knittie said. "We're going to go straight around there when I've finished here for the day."

"I see. Won't most people get changed when they get there?"

"That's what I told Annabel," Jingles said.

"What have I told you, Jingles? It's Knittie when we're in costume. It's important to stay in character."

"Sorry, Knittie, but I did say that it would probably be best if we changed when we got there. I attracted some very strange looks on my way in."

"Show Jill your party piece."

"Jill doesn't want to see it."

He was dead right; I didn't.

"Go on," Knittie insisted. "Show her."

Jingles sighed, and then the next thing I knew, the toecaps of both of his ginormous shoes flipped open, and out popped two little windmills that began to spin around.

"Isn't that great?" Knittie gushed.

"Fantastic. While I think about it, there's something I need to tell you."

"Have you decided to sign up for the clown school too?"

"No, why would I do that? Do you remember I said I'd be setting on an office manager?"

"Yes, dear?"

"I've now appointed someone: Alistair."

"When will he start?"

"A week on Monday."

"Right. Do you think he'll be interested in joining the clown school?"

"I wouldn't think so."

There was only so much clowning around I could take, so I left Knittie and Jingles to it, and went through to my office.

"How could you?" Winky bawled at me.

"How could I *what*?"

"I heard what you said to the old bag lady. You've set on an office manager, and you didn't even have the good grace to give me an interview. You promised you would."

Oh bum!

"There's a very good reason for that."

"Go on." He began to tap his paw. "I'm listening."

"I decided that the office manager job was too junior a position for someone with your abilities."

"That may be true, but still—"

"I thought you'd fit in better in the position of—err—head of strategic planning."

"What would that entail, exactly?"

"Strategic planning of course. While I'm busy on the day-to-day stuff, I need someone who can look at the big picture."

"Blue-sky thinking, you mean?"

"Absolutely."

"You want someone who can think outside the box."

"Outside of the box, inside the box, on top of the box—

all of that stuff."

"That is kind of my forte."

"Exactly what I was thinking."

"Where would I fit in the hierarchy, vis-a-vis the office manager? Would he report to me, or would you expect me to report to him?"

"Neither. You'd be working on parallel but separate paths."

"I like the sound of that."

Phew. "I thought you would."

"There'll be the question of salary of course."

"Obviously, and we'll address that in due course."

"Will I get my own business cards?"

"I think I can run to that."

Chapter 15

The next morning when I came down for breakfast, Jack was seated at the kitchen table, scribbling notes onto an A4 pad.

"Please tell me you haven't started writing poetry too."

"What?" He was clearly too engrossed in whatever he was doing to have heard what I said.

"I thought maybe reading Rhymes' poems had inspired you to write your own."

"No, I'm just making notes of ideas for TenPinCon."

"I should have known."

"Tony said the con was your idea."

"I was only joking when I suggested it."

"I'm really excited about it. They've appointed me as their creative director."

"Will you get paid?"

"No, of course not. It's an honour to be involved in such a prestigious event. You should get involved too."

"I already have enough on my plate, thanks. I've got to give a talk at Mikey's school this afternoon."

"I'd forgotten about that. You should read me what you have prepared."

"I thought I'd just wing it."

"I'm surprised he didn't ask me to give the talk. Most kids are fascinated by policemen."

"It seems not. Apparently, I'm the exciting one in this family. By the way, how did you get on with Rhymes' poetry? Did you speak to your colleague about getting it published?"

"Yes, but I wish I hadn't."

"Why?"

"Richie, that's the guy I mentioned to you, assumed that I'm really Robert Hymes and that the poems are mine, so now everyone in the station is calling me Byron."

"Oh dear." I grinned. "But did he say he could help?"

"Yes. I assume you want paperbacks, not e-books?"

"Yeah. Rhymes just wants one for himself and a few to give away to his friends."

"Richie said he'd get back to me today with some idea of cost. Who's going to be paying for these anyway?"

"Rhymes, of course."

"Do tortoises have money?"

"If he's anything like Winky, he will. That cat's rolling in it. Speaking of whom, he overheard me telling Mrs V that I'd appointed an office manager."

"I bet that went down well."

"Like a lead balloon, but I managed to talk him around. I told him that I was appointing him my head of strategic planning."

"What's that?"

"I've no idea. I made it up on the spur of the moment, but it seems to have placated him."

Jack glanced down at his notes. "What do you think about this idea? We could get a few people to dress up as pins, and then the visitors to the con could pay to try and knock them over with a giant ball."

"Fantastic."

"You could be one of the pins if you like?"

"Gee, thanks. I think I'll pass on that one."

When I'd finished my breakfast, Jack was still busy scribbling notes and smiling to himself.

"I'd better get going." I grabbed my bag. "I just hope

the office isn't full of clowns again today."

"Why would it be?"

"I didn't tell you last night, did I?" Mrs V and Armi have signed up for the clown school. She spent all yesterday at her desk dressed as Knittie the clown."

"Sounds like fun. You and I should sign up too."

"Never. Going. To. Happen."

***

Much to my relief, Mrs V was back behind her desk; there was no sign of her alter ego, Knittie.

"Morning, Mrs V. It's good to see you back to yourself."

"Morning, Jill. I'm afraid you won't be seeing Knittie again for a couple of weeks."

Result! "Oh dear. Why's that?"

"Jingles had a bit of a mishap on his way home last night."

"What happened?"

"When we called in at the mall on the way home, Jingles' shoes got caught on the escalator."

"Is he okay?"

"He sprained his ankle trying to get it loose, but it could have been so much worse."

"Poor Armi."

"Lesson learned. It probably would have been better if we'd changed in and out of our costumes at the school."

"I seem to recall that Armi said that."

"I know, and he isn't letting me forget it."

"Any messages?"

"Yes, two. The first one was from Mr Song, checking that you were happy with the sign. I told him you were."

"Right, and the other?"

"Mr Macabre rang to say he'd be calling in this afternoon."

"Did he say what it was about?"

"I asked, but he wouldn't tell me."

"Great. That'll be something to look forward to."

Winky was standing in front of a large whiteboard, which was covered in lots of lines, boxes, arrows and indecipherable text.

"What are you up to?"

"The revolution has begun." He puffed out his chest. "Prepare to be amazed."

"It's a bit early in the day for quadratic equations. I haven't had any caffeine yet."

"These aren't equations. This is stage one of an eight-part plan to revolutionise this business." He tapped the board. "Look!"

"I see lots of words, but none of them make a lick of sense."

"Allow me to talk you through it."

"Err, I'd love you to, but there's somewhere I need to be."

"When can we do it, then?"

"Soon. Very soon. I promise."

Oh bum! I had hoped that Winky would be satisfied with having a fancy title. I hadn't expected him to actually take the role seriously. Me and my bright ideas.

***

The two men whose wives had been taken back to

Candlefield by Royston Rhodes had met their partners through the Crystal Dating Agency, which was based in a small office in Carnaby Street. It all felt like too much of a coincidence, and certainly warranted further investigation.

Although I wasn't exactly famous, my face was known in certain witch circles, and I'd appeared in the pages of The Candle more times than I would have liked—most recently when I'd thrown away my chance of winning the Elite Competition. I didn't want to risk being recognised, so I would have to change my appearance before visiting the agency. Whose face could I borrow for an hour or so?

Kathy's would do.

When I arrived at the address I'd been given, I was surprised to find that the name on the door read Magical Love Dating Agency.

The door was locked, so I pressed the buzzer.

"Hello?" A female voice crackled through the intercom.

"Hi. I was actually looking for the Crystal Dating Agency."

"We've taken over their business, and we've had a total rebrand. Would you still like to come up?"

"Err, yes please."

Moments later, the door's lock released, and I made my way upstairs.

"Come in." The young witch behind the desk had the most beautiful blue eyes. "I'm Melanie."

"Kathy Brooks."

"Have a seat, Kathy. Would you like a drink?"

"Not for me, thanks. When did you take over from the previous owner?"

"Only a couple of months ago. How did you hear about the agency?"

"Through a friend who used them."

"We provide pretty much the same service as Crystal used to offer, and you'll be pleased to know our rates are a little lower than theirs were."

"That's great."

"I have to ask, Kathy, have you given serious thought to the implications of finding a human partner?"

"Err, yes. I think so."

"I sincerely hope so because it's a very serious step. You realise that you would never be able to reveal to your partner that you're a witch."

"Yes, of course."

"Keeping a secret like that isn't something everyone can do. You'd essentially be living a lie for the rest of your life. Do you think you could manage that?"

"Yes, I'm sure I could. If I found the right person."

"Great. I'll just need to take a few details."

"Okay."

She spent the next thirty minutes or so asking questions about me, and the kind of partner I was looking for.

"That's pretty much everything, Kathy. All we need now is a couple of photos."

"Don't you want me to prove that I'm a witch?"

"No, of course not." She was clearly surprised by the question. "I can see you are."

"It's just that one of my friends told me they had to do that before Crystal would take them onto their books."

"How very strange." She hesitated. "But that could explain some of the video clips I found."

"What clips?"

"Sorry, I was just thinking out loud."

"What was on them?"

"Why are you so interested anyway?"

It was time to come clean, so I reversed the spell that was masking my true identity.

"I'm sorry for the deception."

"I don't understand. What's going on? Don't I know you from somewhere?"

"My real name is Jill Maxwell. It's possible you know me as Jill Gooder."

"Of course. It's an honour to meet you, but I still don't understand what this is all about."

"I have reason to believe that whoever was running the Crystal Dating Agency was tricking its clients into performing magic, supposedly to prove they were witches. In fact, they were secretly videoing them. If the witch subsequently found a partner and married, the video would be sent to their husband."

"Why would they do something like that?"

"I'm afraid I can't discuss that. At least, not until the people behind this outrage are brought to justice."

"I understand. Is there anything I can do to help?"

"You could start by telling me about the video clips you found."

"Sure. When I was having a clear-out of the stuff the previous owner left behind, I came across an old computer. I thought it was broken, but when I switched it on, it worked. There was nothing much on it, but I did find a few video clips of witches performing spells. I must admit, I didn't think much of it at the time."

"Do you still have them?"

"I'm afraid not. The computer was really old, so I threw

it away."

"That's a pity, but never mind. If you could just give me the name of the person who you bought the agency from, that would be a great help."

***

Back at the office, Winky now had a second whiteboard on the go.

"I'm glad you're back." He put the marker pen down. "We have a lot to get through."

"So I see. Unfortunately, it will have to wait because the landlord will be here at any minute. You'll need to hide behind the screen."

"Do I have to?"

"It's either that or I make you invisible."

"Fine, I'll go behind the screen, but try to get rid of him quickly, will you?"

"I'll do my best."

Mrs V showed Macabre into my office, but didn't offer him a drink.

"Mr Macabre, you're here again. I'm beginning to think you have a crush on me."

"Hmm." He looked over at the two whiteboards. "That looks rather complicated. What is it?"

"That's err—my new strategy for the business. I've been doing a little blue-sky thinking."

"Really?" He moved closer to the two boards. "What's this box here?"

"Synergy. I intend to maximise it. Maximum synergy, that's the plan."

"I see. It all looks rather complicated."

"Not when you understand this stuff. Anyway, you said you wanted to see me?"

"Indeed I do. I'm sorry to tell you that you are in breach of your lease." He didn't look very sorry. In fact, it was the first time he'd smiled since he'd walked into the room.

"What do you mean? If you're still banging on about me running a clock business, I—"

"It's not that. This time there's no doubt you're in breach."

"How am I?"

"Clause 32A, sub-section iv is quite clear."

"Clear about what?"

"That each tenant may display one sign on the exterior of the building."

"Yes? So?"

"You have not one, but two signs on the wall outside."

"Err—yes, but it's really only a single sign. It's just that it's in two parts."

"This really is very simple. If you don't remove one of your signs, I'll be forced to evict you from these offices for breach of contract."

"You can't do that."

"I think you'll find I can."

"I'll need some time to sort it out."

"Of course. I'm a reasonable man. You have until five o'clock on Friday." Still grinning, he made his way to the door. "It's been a pleasure, as always."

"Right, then." Winky came out from behind the screen. "Are you ready for my presentation?"

"I can't do it now."

"But you promised."

"That was before I knew I had a sign emergency on my hands."

"You should just ignore Macabre. He's all wind and trousers."

"I daren't ignore him. He's been looking for an opportunity to get me out, and this is just the excuse he needs." I picked up the phone and made a call.

"Mr Song?"

"Sid Song singing."

"Do you have to do that?"

"Do what? Is that Jill Maxwell?"

"Yes, it is. The singing? Is it really necessary? Never mind. It's about the sign."

"Your PA told me you were pleased with the end result."

"I was."

"Excellent."

"But I need you to take it down now."

"Sorry? You just this minute said you were happy with it?"

"I am, but my landlord isn't. It seems that under the terms of my lease, I'm only allowed to display a single sign."

"Didn't you know that before you —"

"Obviously I didn't, or I wouldn't have done it."

"There's no need to bite my head off."

"Sorry, I'm a little stressed at the moment. Here's what I want you to do: Come and take down the second sign immediately. Then make me a new sign that includes the wording from the two existing signs, and finally replace the first sign with the new sign."

"I can remove the sign—that's no problem, but it'll be a couple of weeks at least before I can supply the replacement."

"How come? You managed to fit Clown in straight away."

"They just happened to fall lucky. I'd had a cancellation."

"Okay, I guess I'll just have to wait. But you must make sure you take down that second sign before five on Friday."

"No problem. Leave it with me."

Chapter 16

I made it to the school with only five minutes to spare. A very worried Mikey was standing just inside the main doors.

"I didn't think you were coming, Auntie Jill. The other parents have been here for ages."

"Other parents?"

"Come on!" He grabbed me by the hand and dragged me down the corridor.

"Where are we going?"

"To the main hall."

This wasn't what I'd expected. I'd assumed I'd be giving a talk in Mikey's classroom, but there was no time to ask questions because we were already in the hall.

I was only too aware that class sizes had gradually increased over recent years, but I was pretty sure they hadn't grown to this number. The hall was full of children and teachers.

"Mikey." I pulled him to one side. "I thought I was just going to be speaking to your class?"

"Mrs Maxwell?" A man came rushing towards me.

"Err, yeah?"

"We didn't think you were coming. Follow me, please."

I had no choice but to do as he said. He led the way to the front of the hall, and through a small door that was clearly the stage entrance.

"Excuse me." I grabbed his arm. "I'm a little confused. I thought I was giving a talk to my nephew's class."

"No, you'll be speaking to the whole school. The pupils in each class were asked to nominate their parent or another relative to speak about the job they do. All the pupils in the school then voted on which three they most wanted to hear. I believe you topped the poll. It's quite an honour, really."

"I guess so."

"You do have something prepared, I assume?"

"Err—yes, of course."

"There are two others to speak before you."

"Right." He started up the steps towards the stage. "Just one more thing. Do you know what the others do for a living?"

"Let me see." He checked the notes he had with him. "Wendy Middleton will be speaking about her work in the Third World. She works with children affected by famine. Michael West will be giving a talk on his work helping to save polar bears."

"Right."

The next thing I knew, I was seated at the rear of the stage, in-between a man and a woman, who I assumed to be the other speakers.

How had I managed to land myself in this mess? It was all Mikey's fault—he hadn't made it clear that I'd be giving a talk to the whole school, and he certainly hadn't told me that I would have to follow two speakers who had devoted their lives to such worthy causes.

The headmaster called for silence.

"Boys and girls. We are very lucky to have three people with us today who have given up their precious time in order to talk to you about the important work they do." He consulted his notes. "First, we have Mrs Middleton who works tirelessly to help the disadvantaged children of the Third World. Following her will be Mr West who is involved in the fight to save the polar bear from extinction. And finally, we have Mrs Maxwell." He glanced again at his papers. "No doubt, she'll be able to explain what she does. So, without further ado, please welcome your first speaker, Mrs Middleton."

Wendy Middleton took to the podium, and immediately called for the lights to be dimmed. Not only had she prepared a fascinating and very moving presentation, she'd also put together a slideshow to accompany it. When she'd finished, there was barely a dry eye in the house—I had to accept a tissue from Michael West.

When it was his turn to take to the podium, he too asked for the lights to be dimmed. There was a short movie to accompany his presentation, and needless to say, his talk went down a storm—what wasn't to love about polar bears?

"Thank you, Mr West," the headmaster said. "That was fascinating. And finally, I'm delighted to invite Mrs Maxwell to give her presentation. Please give her a huge round of applause."

Try to imagine how I felt. How was I supposed to follow those excellent presentations given by two people who had devoted their whole lives to good causes? Even if I'd had the foresight to prepare notes, anything I had to say would have sounded shallow by comparison.

Are you familiar with the saying *I wish the ground would swallow me up*?

I had to time the spells just right, otherwise I could have done myself a serious injury. The first spell caused the stage to crack underneath my feet. As I fell through the hole, I cast the 'levitate' spell to ensure a soft landing.

"Mrs Maxwell!" The headmaster looked down through

the hole in the stage. "Are you alright down there?"

Apart from being covered in dust, I was perfectly fine, but I couldn't let him know that.

"Ouch, I think so."

"I'll call an ambulance."

By now, several people were gathered above me on the stage, all peering through the hole.

"There's no need to do that." I got to my feet and brushed myself down. "Nothing seems to be broken. Just a few scrapes and bruises."

"Thank goodness."

I wasn't sure if the headmaster's concern was for my wellbeing or for the potential legal claim that might have ensued.

"I'm afraid I won't be able to give my talk, though. I'm feeling a little shaken."

"Perfectly understandable. Stay right where you are, and I'll have someone take you to my office. A hot cup of tea is what's called for."

"Thanks. Do you happen to have any biscuits or cake to go with that? I feel as though I need sugar right now."

"Of course. I'll see to it straight away."

By the time Mikey came to see me in the headmaster's office, I was on my third Jaffa Cake. They were a poor substitute for custard creams, but beggars can't be choosers.

"Are you okay, Auntie Jill?" He looked genuinely concerned.

"I'm fine, thanks. I'm sorry that I wasn't able to give my talk. I've been really looking forward to it."

"That's okay. All of my friends thought the way you fell

through the stage was brill."

***

On my way home, I called in at the Corner Shop. Little Jack was boogying down the aisle to a Motown classic, which was blaring out of the speakers.

"Care to dance, Jill?"

"No thanks. I'm not much of a dancer. Is the music new? I don't recall hearing it in here before."

"Yes, I installed the sound system earlier today. I read an article that shoppers are thirty-three per cent more likely to purchase twenty-two per cent more goods if there is in-store music."

"Interesting." That sounded like one-hundred per cent nonsense to me, but I didn't want to burst Jack's bubble.

"Were you satisfied with the home delivery service, Jill?"

"I was, but I'm a little concerned for Lucy. She told me she'd never ridden a bike before."

"Fret not. I have taken steps to ensure Lucy is safe."

"That's good to hear."

"Will you be needing home delivery again today?"

"Not this time. I only need a loaf of bread and some milk."

As I paid for my bits and bobs, Little Jack pointed to the newspaper he'd been reading. "Terrible business about the woman in the canal, isn't it?"

"Sorry?"

"They found a woman's body in the canal this morning."

"Do you mind if I take a look at that?"

"Help yourself."

The article in The Bugle was short on detail, but confirmed that the body of a young woman had been pulled from Washbridge Canal, about a mile downstream from where Pam Turton's boat had been moored at the time she went missing.

As I headed out of the shop, I bumped into Lucy Locket.

"Hi, Jill."

"Little Jack tells me that he's taken steps to ensure your safety on the bike. Has he sent you on a cycling proficiency course?"

"Not exactly. Come and look." She led me around the back of the shop to where her bike was parked.

"Stabilisers?"

***

When I pulled onto the drive, Britt and Kit were out front. At first glance, it appeared that he was trying to calm her down.

"Is everything okay?" I said.

"She'll be alright." Kit nodded.

"No one believes me," she blubbed. "Everyone thinks I'm going crazy, but I know what I saw."

"Britt thinks the trees are moving around." He rolled his eyes.

"I know what I saw." She pushed him away. "That tree was in the garden over the road when I came home from work, and now it's in Jill's garden."

I couldn't let the poor woman suffer like this.

"You're absolutely right, Britt."

"What?" Kit looked shocked by my response.

"I'm sorry, Britt. I should have told you earlier."

"Told me what?" She wiped her eyes.

I turned to the tree. "Mr Hosey, I think you'd better show yourself."

A small slot appeared in the tree trunk, through which Mr Hosey's eyes, nose and mouth were visible. "I'm very sorry, young lady, I didn't mean to cause you any upset."

"What's going on?" Kit demanded.

I thought I'd better speak up before Kit punched Hosey on the nose. "Mr Hosey is chairman of the neighbourhood watch committee. As you can see, he takes his duties extremely seriously. The tree is his latest surveillance aid."

"I wish someone had warned us." Kit was still fuming.

"It's okay." Britt was smiling now. "I'm just glad I'm not going crazy." She turned to the Hosey tree. "Do you happen to have a bush too?"

"I certainly do. I call it Bramble, and this is Barker."

"I'm sorry I didn't say anything before, Britt," I said. "I didn't want to blow Mr Hosey's cover."

"That's okay. It's kind of comforting to know we have someone looking out for our properties."

Jack was already home and had made a start on dinner.

"Something smells nice." I sniffed the air.

"It should be ready in about twenty minutes."

"Did you hear about the body they found in the canal?"

"Yeah, I saw it on the local news when I checked the bowling scores."

"Could you find out if they've identified it yet?"

"You know I can't do that, Jill."

"Not even if I promise to come up with the best afters you've ever had?"

"No. This is precisely why I got the transfer to West Chipping. I won't be your inside man. You'll have to do your own digging around."

"I hate incorruptible people."

***

I'd fallen asleep on the sofa, and was enjoying the most fabulous dream when Jack nudged me.

"What's up? I was dreaming that I'd won a year's supply of custard creams."

"That's great, but you just got a text message."

I could see the text had come from an unknown number. If some idiot had disturbed my custard cream dream with some stupid marketing message, I would not be a happy bunny.

It turned out that the text had been generated by the floral fairies' low water level alarm system, which Patch had subscribed me to.

"I have to nip over to Candlefield."

"Are you sure you're awake enough to fly?"

"I don't *fly*. Why would you think I fly?"

"I thought that's what happened when you use magic to travel back and forth between here and Candlefield."

"On my broom, I assume?"

"How am I supposed to know how it works?"

"I certainly don't fly there, with or without a broom."

"Why do you have to go, anyway?"

"The floral fairies reservoir levels are dangerously low."

He gave me a kiss. "Just be careful."

"I always am. See you in two ticks."

The arrangement was that I should magic myself straight to Hyacinth House. When I arrived there, Patch was waiting for me. Butter was there too.

"There's really no need for you to come, your majesty," Patch said.

"I want to see this for myself," she insisted.

"But Peg can only manage two on her back."

"Why don't I magic us all there?" I suggested.

"That's an excellent idea," Butter said.

Patch looked less than enthusiastic, but he wasn't about to argue with his queen.

We went directly to the west plantation, which Patch and I had visited only the day before. The sight that met us was horrifying — the reservoir was bone dry.

"This is even worse than I thought." Butter looked visibly shaken.

"It makes no sense, your majesty," Patch walked over to the edge of the reservoir. "The level was low yesterday when Jill was here, but there's no way this should have happened in twenty-four hours."

"Could there be a blockage upstream?" Butter looked at the hillside beyond the reservoir.

"There wasn't when I last checked."

"Let's double-check." Butter started towards the hill, with Patch and me in close pursuit.

Patch was the only one of us dressed for the terrain, but I didn't feel I should complain because Butter showed no sign of turning back.

An hour later, we'd reached the top of the hill. We were all exhausted and covered in mud and nettle stings.

"There's nothing," Butter said while still trying to catch

her breath. "The stream is flowing normally."

We took a five-minute break, and then made our way back down. It was easier going, but just as muddy. By the time we made it back to the reservoir, it was slowly starting to refill from the stream, but it would be a long time before it reached the level needed to service the meadows of flowers.

"There's obviously nothing wrong with the supply of water to the reservoir," Butter said. "Someone or something must be emptying the water once it gets in here." She turned to me. "Any ideas, Jill?"

"I wish I did, but at the moment, I have no clue what is happening."

"But you'll stay on the case, won't you?"

"Of course."

"I'm relying on you. If this continues, it will be catastrophic for my people."

No pressure then.

"Where on earth have you been?" Jack looked horrified, and so he might. If I'd had my wits about me, I could have made sure I landed outside of the house. Instead I was standing in the lounge, covered in mud.

Chapter 17

The next morning, I was first out of the door.

I usually made a point of having the correct change ready for the toll bridge, but Jack had been bending my ear all morning about TenPinCon, and I'd forgotten to get the cash out of my purse.

"Sorry, I won't be a minute," I shouted towards the toll booth, as I grabbed my handbag from the passenger seat.

"No hurry," said a familiar voice.

"Mr Ivers?"

"Morning, Jill." He beamed. "I bet you didn't expect to see me here."

"You're right. I was a little worried when you did a moonlight flit. Are you alright?"

"Never better. I'm sorry I left without a word. I suppose I was a little embarrassed, but I've had time to think about things now, and I'm much happier with life."

"And you have your old job back?"

"Yes. It seems they find it difficult to retain good people, so when I contacted them, they welcomed me back with open arms."

"I'm sorry your business ventures didn't pan out."

"There's no point in dwelling on that. I've learned a lot about myself since I won the money. First and foremost, I'm not suited to the cut and thrust of running my own business. I'm more of a worker bee, I suppose."

"There's nothing wrong with that."

"And secondly, I've realised what's really important to me is my love of movies. I abandoned them for a while, but now that I don't have the pressure of running my own business, I intend to pick up where I left off."

"Good for you. It's great that you have such a positive attitude."

"You'll be pleased to hear that I've decided to revive my movie newsletter."

Oh bum! "That's fantastic."

"Needless to say, I've re-instated your subscription. You must have been missing your regular update."

"Well, actually—"

"I know what you're going to say, but there's no need to worry because I won't be hiking the price. It will be the same subscription fee as you were paying before."

"But, I—"

Someone in the long queue of traffic behind me sounded their horn.

"It's okay, Jill. You can pay me when the first newsletter is published. It should be next week with a bit of luck."

"Great!"

*****

Although I was relieved to find Mr Ivers was alive and well, I really wished he'd found employment elsewhere. The thought of having to put up with him every day, on my way back and forth to work, was enough to make me consider using magic instead of the car.

As I walked from the car park, I received a call from Kathy.

"I hear you brought the house down yesterday at Mikey's school." She laughed.

"I'm fine. Thanks for asking."

"It could only happen to you."

"Did you call just to have a laugh at my expense?"

"Mainly, yes, but I also wanted to ask you to come over to see the new shop. The shop fitters have finished and the sign is up."

"Already? That was quick."

"I was lucky. That guy you put me onto, Sid Song, was able to do me a rush job."

"Was he? That's nice." He could do it for everyone apart from me, apparently.

"So, will you pop over?"

"What time?"

"I'll be there from about midday."

"I can't promise, but if I get the chance I'll come over."

"Okay. Oh, and Jill."

"Yes."

"Watch your step. Don't go falling down any holes."

"You're so funny."

***

"Hi!" said the young woman who I bumped into on the way into my office building. "What's your name?"

"I'm Jill."

"No, I meant your clown name. I'm Sausage."

"I'm not actually here for the clown school. My offices are in this building too."

"Sorry. I just assumed."

"No problem."

"The school is really fantastic."

"I'm sure it is."

"I've always been shy and nervous around people, but when I'm Sausage, it's like I become another person. Do you know what I mean?"

"Sort of. Anyway, I'd better get inside. Lots to do."

"Bye then, Jill."

"Bye, err—Sausage."

"Who's Sausage?" Mrs V said.

I didn't answer because I was too distracted by what was going on behind her desk. Half a dozen clowns were gathered around the cupboard, looking at some kind of brochure.

"What are *they* doing in here?" I said in a hushed voice.

"They're some of the clowns I met next door. Someone asked why I'd chosen my clown name, and I explained that I was a keen knitter. The next thing I knew, everyone was asking if I could knit them some clown socks. They're picking out patterns and colours."

"I didn't realise there was such a thing as clown socks."

"BoBo!" She called one of the clowns over. "Show Jill your clown socks."

"My pleasure." He honked the horn in his hand, and then proceeded to roll up his trouser legs. "See."

"Very nice. So, essentially, clown socks are just very long socks, in a ridiculous combination of colours?"

"And, of course, they must be odd," Mrs V said.

"Right. And will you be charging them for the socks?"

"Of course not. It will be my contribution to the clown community."

"That's very generous." And, in my opinion, a golden opportunity missed.

"Would you like some, Jill?"

"Clown socks? I don't think so."

"They're very warm. Ideal for cold winter days."

"I'll stick to my woolly tights, thanks."

The whiteboard count had now increased to three. If this carried on, I soon wouldn't be able to squeeze into my office.

"You'll be pleased to know my original eight-part plan has now become a more comprehensive ten-part plan." Winky tapped the third whiteboard.

I was beginning to regret my decision to give him the made-up job title.

"Are you paying attention?" he snapped.

"Err, yeah. Will this take long?"

"Three hours max."

"*Three hours?*"

Just as he was about to launch into the presentation, my phone rang.

"You should have turned that thing off," he scolded.

"Sorry. I'd better take it now."

"Is that Jill?" Although I recognised Jane Bond's voice, I could barely make out what she was saying through her tears.

"Hello, Jane. How are you?"

"Not great. You've already heard, I take it?"

"I knew they'd found a woman's body, but I wasn't sure—"

"It's Pam. I've just identified her."

"I'm so very sorry."

"Thank you. I've called about the work you've been doing."

"Don't worry. I won't be billing you."

"It's not that. I rang to say I'd like you to find out who did this terrible thing."

"Have the police confirmed it was murder?"

"Yes."

"In that case, they'll be carrying out their own investigation. There's no need for you to pay me to investigate too."

"I want to. If the police had taken notice when I tried to report her missing, then maybe—" Her words trailed away.

"Jane? Are you sure about this?"

"Positive." She blew her nose. "And besides, you already have a head start on them."

"Okay. Are you going to be alright?"

"I will be when the scumbag who did this is brought to justice."

When I got off the phone, Winky was glaring at me.

"I'm sorry, but I had to take that. It was important."

"So is this." He tapped each of the whiteboards. "The future of your business is at stake."

"Okay, I'm all yours now."

At that very moment, the door to my office flew open, and in stormed my BFF, Sue Shay. Fortunately, she was so busy glaring at me that she didn't notice Winky toss the board marker across the room in frustration.

"Hello, Sue. Long time, no see. I was beginning to think you'd gone off me."

"It's still Detective Shay to you."

"Can I get you something to drink? Probably best to steer clear of caffeine. Your blood pressure looks like it's high enough already."

"I don't want a drink, but what I do want is an explanation."

"About your high blood pressure? That's a very

complex subject."

"One more smart remark from you, and we'll be having this conversation back at the station."

"You're going to have to give me a clue. What is it you want to discuss?"

"As if you didn't already know. How is it when I started to ask questions about the woman whose body was found in Washbridge Canal, people told me you'd already been noseying around?"

"When I was asking questions about Pam Turton, I believed that she was still alive. I was working a missing person case. Would you like to know why her sister brought the case to me?"

"I get the feeling you're going to tell me anyway."

"Your people weren't interested because she'd run away a few times as a kid, so they decided no action was necessary."

"What did you find out? I want everything you know."

I had no reason to hold anything back, so I told Shay about the burglaries and my discussions with the Trumans and Suki Coates. I also told her about Pam's ex, Josh Radford.

"Is that everything?"

"There's CCTV on some stretches of the canal, but the Canal Authority weren't prepared to let me view it. It might be worth checking that."

"Thanks, but I don't need you to tell me how to suck eggs."

"I was just trying to —"

"Well don't. Now that this is an official murder investigation, I don't expect to see you anywhere near it. Is that clear?"

"Crystal."

"I'm sorry about that, Jill." Mrs V came through to my office. "I tried to stop her, but you know what she's like."

"It's okay."

"I heard that they'd found a woman's body in the canal. Was it—?"

"Pam Turton? Yes, I'm afraid so. Her sister called me just before Shay turned up. She wants me to try to find the murderer."

"Didn't Shay just tell you to stay away from the case?"

"Did she? I must have missed that."

Fortunately, Winky was so fed up of waiting to give his presentation that he'd fallen asleep under the sofa.

What a pity. I'd so been looking forward to that.

***

You'd think I'd learn, wouldn't you, but no.

Yesterday, I'd turned up at Mikey's school without doing a lick of preparation. Today, I was supposed to be talking to the Witches Of Washbridge, better known as W.O.W. I'd only agreed to do it because I'd been strong-armed by Grandma who was chairman of the organisation. It still rankled that I was apparently good enough to give a talk, but not good enough to warrant an invitation to join this mysterious group.

First, though, I had to find their new HQ: W.O.W. Central.

Grandma had told me that I should take the north road from the marketplace, and keep walking. According to her, you couldn't miss it.

Apparently, *I* could.

I'd been walking along the north road for almost twenty minutes, but I still hadn't seen W.O.W. Central.

"There you are!" I turned around to find Grandma running up behind me. She was red in the face, and looked about ready to collapse. "Where do you think you're going?"

"I'm looking for your new HQ."

"You passed it ten minutes ago." She was bent double, trying to catch her breath.

"I don't see how I could have missed it. I looked at every building on both sides of the road."

"Did you remember to cast the 'true reveal' spell?"

"The what?"

"Some witch you are. I told you that you'd need to cast the 'true reveal' spell to see the building."

"That's not what you said. You told me—"

"There's no time for your jibber jabber. You're already ten minutes late. You do realise that this will reflect badly on me, don't you?"

"I'm sorry, but I still say—"

"Never mind." She grabbed my hand, and dragged me back down the street.

En route, she showed me the 'true reveal' spell, which I'd never even heard of until then. Essentially, it was the antidote to the 'mask' spell, which had been used to disguise W.O.W. Central, for reasons that completely eluded me.

When I'd walked past it the first time, the building had appeared to be an ice cream parlour. I remembered because I'd been tempted to nip in and try one. Now, though, I saw the true façade of the HQ.

"It's very impressive," I said.

"Come on!" She dragged me up the stairs and into a large hall which was full of witches. Once we were on the stage, Grandma practically pushed me into a chair, and then took the microphone from its stand. "Ladies, I must apologise once again for the tardiness of my granddaughter. It seems she forgot to cast the 'true reveal' spell."

A few of the audience laughed politely.

I considered correcting Grandma, but decided that, on balance, I'd prefer to keep breathing.

Grandma continued, "The membership requested that Jill give this presentation about growing up as a human. Like me, I'm sure you're looking forward to seeing what she has prepared for us." Oh bum! I was so dead. "Jill, would you step forward and take the mic."

I walked nervously to the front of the stage and took it from her. As I did, she whispered, "This had better be good. If you embarrass me, you'll be sorry."

Gulp.

As I stood there, I could feel the beads of perspiration gathering on my forehead. My mouth was bone dry, and my mind had gone completely blank; I didn't have the first clue what to say. It wasn't the hundreds of expectant faces in the audience that worried me. It was the pair of eyes burning into my back.

"Thank you." I managed. "The subject of this talk is — err —" I couldn't even remember what the stupid subject was.

Just then, a door at the side of the auditorium opened, and a short, stocky witch hurried down the aisle and onto the stage where she whispered something to Grandma.

"Right now?" Grandma boomed.

"Yes, please. It's extremely urgent."

"Very well." Grandma stood up. "I have to leave for a short while. Carry on, Jill."

Once Grandma and the other witch had disappeared out of the hall, I turned back to the audience, but I still didn't have a clue what I was going to talk about.

"The subject of — err — "

"Don't worry about it, Jill." One of the witches in the first row stood up, and made her way onto the stage.

"I'm really sorry about this," I said when she joined me at the mic.

"Don't be. We didn't ask you to come here today to give a talk."

"Sorry? I don't understand. I thought — "

"That was just a ploy so that your grandmother wouldn't know the real reason we wanted you to come."

"And what's that?"

"We want you to be the new chairman of W.O.W."

Chapter 18

"Have you lost your freaking minds?" I glanced across at the door through which Grandma had just disappeared.

"We're deadly serious, I can assure you. I probably should introduce myself. I'm Belinda Cartwheel. For my sins, I've been appointed the spokeswoman, and I can assure you that I speak for all of the witches gathered here today."

"That may be true, but what you're advocating is that I lead some kind of coup. Against my own flesh and blood."

"I realise we're placing you in a difficult position, Jill, but there's no other witch in Candlefield who is strong enough to stand up to your grandmother."

"I don't get it. I've never even been invited to join W.O.W, and now suddenly you want me to lead the organisation?"

"Everyone here wanted you to join. We've been pushing for it to happen for ages, but your grandmother blocked it every time."

"Why would she do that?"

"I believe she's scared of allowing a witch even more powerful than herself into the fold. She probably thinks you'll eventually challenge her position as head of W.O.W."

I glanced again at the door. "Where has she gone?"

"We created a short diversion to allow us to speak to you."

"Couldn't you have approached me somewhere else? This is crazy."

"We thought it important that you saw the strength of

feeling for such a move."

"I'm sorry, but I won't do it. For all her faults, Grandma has been one of the pillars of the witch community for longer than most of you have been alive. I won't be a party to this."

"But, Jill—"

Just then, the door at the side of the auditorium opened, and a witch with long green hair appeared. "They're on their way back."

Belinda Cartwheel hurried off the stage and back to her seat like a bat out of hell.

If I'd been nervous before, it was nothing to the mix of emotions I now felt as I waited for Grandma to return.

"A total waste of my time." Her voice came from just outside the auditorium.

"And so, ladies," I said into the mic. "That's what it was like growing up as a human."

At that moment, two things happened: The audience broke into applause, and Grandma made her way back onto the stage.

"Is that it?" she whispered.

"Yes, it seems to have gone down well, I think."

She looked out over the audience who were now giving me a standing ovation. "A bit on the short side, wasn't it?"

"You know what they say, Grandma. Good things come in small packages."

A few minutes later, the hall was empty except for Grandma and me.

"What do you think of the ladies of W.O.W?" she said.

"Hard to say. I didn't have a chance to speak to anyone."

"It's about time that changed. I think you should join our ranks."

"Are you inviting me to become a member?"

"Why not? I would have suggested it before now, but some of the rank and file are still a little suspicious of you."

"Why?"

"I'd have thought that was obvious. You spent the majority of your life living as a human. That makes some people very nervous. So, what do you say? Will you join us?"

"Yes, I'd like that."

"Good. I won't be around forever. It would be nice to think that you might take over from me, eventually."

"I'm not sure about that. One step at a time."

"Just a word of warning. Most of our ladies are good sorts, but like any organisation, there are a few bad apples. One in particular to look out for is Belinda Cartwheel. I wouldn't trust that one as far as I could throw her."

"Right. I'll bear that in mind."

When I left the HQ, Grandma stayed behind, to catch up on some paperwork.

I'd arranged to meet Daze and Blaze at Cuppy C, and on the walk over there, I tried to make sense of what had just occurred. Should I have told Grandma what had happened while she was out of the hall? And what was I to make of Belinda Cartwheel? Did she really have the backing of all the membership? It had certainly seemed that way at the time.

At least now that I was a member of W.O.W, I'd be able

to make my own assessment of what was happening inside that organisation. Was Grandma really universally disliked, or was there something more sinister afoot?

***

I arrived at Cuppy C ahead of time.

"Hi, Jill." Mindy was all alone behind the counter.

"Hi. No Pearl today?"

"She's working in the cake shop because they're shorthanded. Can I get you anything?"

"I'm actually meeting Daze and Blaze here in a few minutes. I'll wait until they arrive before ordering."

"Okay. Why don't you go and take a look at the creche while you're waiting?"

"Oh yeah. I'd forgotten it had opened this week. How's it going?"

"Very well from all accounts. Amber and Pearl seem delighted."

"I'll take a look. If Daze and Blaze arrive, tell them I'll be down in a few minutes, will you?"

"Sure."

As I made my way upstairs, I expected to be met by a wall of sound, but I didn't hear so much as a peep. Perhaps I'd called during a quiet period?

But no. Far from it. The creche was doing a roaring trade. In fact, there were more customers upstairs than downstairs. And yet, the room was practically silent except for the sound of the occasional cup against saucer.

At least a dozen toddlers were in the centre of the room, all seemingly engrossed in the toys in front of them.

Meanwhile, their parents, mostly mothers, were seated around the edge of the room on large, colourful, padded benches.

It was a charming scene, but something about it struck me as odd. None of the children were shouting, screaming or crying. Even more unusual: There were no arguments over toys; the kids all seemed content to play quietly with their own toy. Just as curious was that none of the parents were talking, either to one another or to their children. Instead, they sat quietly, enjoying their drinks.

"Hello again, Jill."

I almost jumped out of my skin because I hadn't noticed that Belladonna was standing behind me.

"Hi. How's it going?"

"Very well, I think. The twins seem pleased. We've been busy since the moment we opened on Monday."

"I'm a little surprised at how quiet it is up here. I'd expected pandemonium."

She smiled. "I'm a great believer that a calm atmosphere is important for both the children and parents."

"You've certainly achieved that."

Just then, one of the mothers stood up and collected her youngster. "Come on, Tiffany. It's time to go."

This would be the true test. Children hated being separated from their toys, and I fully expected the child to kick off.

"Okay, Mummy." The little girl returned the toy to the box, and then took her mother's hand.

"See you again soon, Tiffany." Belladonna gave a little wave.

After mother and daughter had left, I took my leave too. "I'd better get back downstairs."

"Bye, Jill."

Daze and Blaze were already seated by the door.

"We've got yours, Jill," Blaze called to me. "Caramel latte and a blueberry muffin. I hope that's okay?"

Result!

"Thanks. How much do I owe you?"

"My treat." Daze waved away my offer to pay.

Double result!

"How are you holding up, Daze?" I took a bite of muffin.

"I've had better days." She forced a smile.

"Hopefully, what I have to tell you will make you feel a whole lot better."

"What have you got, Jill?" Blaze said.

"I've spoken to two of the rogue retrievers who worked with Royston Rhodes in London: Bazaar and Radar."

"I know them." Daze nodded. "Good guys, both of them."

"They were keen to help, but neither of them had any dirt on Rhodes that I could use. There was something that Bazaar said that struck me as strange, though."

I went on to tell them about Rhodes' unusual arrest pattern, which comprised almost entirely of witches who had revealed their secret to their partners.

"I've never heard of anything like that," Daze said. "I wouldn't have thought it was possible."

"That's what Radar and Bazaar said too. That's why I followed it up by speaking to two of the men whose wives had been taken back to Candlefield."

"You must have had to reveal you were a witch in order to do that," Daze said.

"I did. I had no choice."

"You shouldn't have taken that kind of risk for me."

"Why not? You're only in this mess because of me. And besides, if Rhodes prevails against you, how long do you think it will be before he comes after me?"

"I would never give you up, Jill."

"I know that, but Rhodes doesn't strike me as the sort to let it go. Anyway, as I was saying, I talked to these two men, and I found out they had something very unusual in common."

I explained to Daze and Blaze how the witches' secret had been revealed, not by loose tongues, but by video clips sent anonymously to their husbands.

"Are you saying Rhodes was behind the videos?" Blaze asked.

"Indirectly, yes, but he had an accomplice. I traced the videos to the same dating agency used by both witches. Would you care to guess who owned that dating agency?"

"Surely not Rhodes?"

"No. His wife, Arabella Rhodes. As soon as her husband secured the promotion he was after, she sold up and moved out."

Daze no longer looked defeated. Instead, she looked angry enough to kill someone. "Let me get this straight, Jill. You're telling me that Rhodes created the offences, which he then took credit for clearing up?"

"That's right. None of the witches he arrested had done anything wrong. They weren't the ones who had revealed their secret. That was down to the videos that Rhodes sent to their partners. The only mistake they made was to use the Crystal Dating Agency."

"I'm going to tear him limb from limb!" Daze stood up.

"Don't do anything silly." I grabbed her by the arm and pulled her back into the seat. "There's more than enough evidence to put him away for a very long time."

"You're right, Jill. And doing so will give me enormous pleasure. I don't know how to thank you."

"No thanks are necessary. I owe you this and much more."

Daze and Blaze couldn't wait to get started on their mission to see Rhodes behind bars. They left in such a hurry that Daze hadn't even touched her muffin.

What? It would have been a waste to just leave it lying there.

As I made my way out of the shop, I almost fell over a young child who had broken free from her mother's hand.

"Come here, Tiffany!"

"Won't! Won't! Won't!" She stamped her feet. "Don't like you!"

The woman looked slightly embarrassed, as she took the child by the hand. "I'm very sorry about this."

"No problem."

As the woman led the child away, the youngster was still screaming blue murder. It was only then that it struck me: this was the same child I'd seen in the creche. The little angel who'd been playing quietly, and who'd put away her toy as soon as her mother had asked her to.

***

I magicked myself over to West Chipping. Just as Kathy had mentioned on the phone, her new sign had been installed.

"You made it." She had to unlock the door to let me in.

"I said I would if I could."

"What do you think of it?"

The shopfitters had worked wonders in the little time they'd had.

"It looks great, and at least now I understand the name."

"What do you mean?"

"It's Kathy's Bridal Shop Two."

"That's what I said."

"Yes, but I thought you meant Kathy's Bridal Shop too."

"Let's not do this again."

"Yes, let's not."

"The stock should be arriving over the next few days."

"So when do you open?"

"Now that I have my manager, I'm hoping to open the week after next."

"You've set someone on?"

"Yeah. Sorry, I meant to let you know, but things have been so hectic that it completely slipped my mind. Pippa was every bit as impressive as you said she'd be. She starts next Monday."

"Fantastic."

"By the way, with all of this going on, are you still going to be able to make it on Saturday?"

"I really should work, but stuff it. If Pete can take the day off to go fishing, then I can have a girly day with you."

"I don't do *girly*."

"Well, I do. Where do you want to go for lunch?"

"I don't know. I'll give it some thought. Somewhere ridiculously expensive."

"Weren't you working on that case with the woman on the boat who was murdered?"

"Yeah. I still am."

"I just heard on the local news that the police are appealing for anyone who has seen an ex-boyfriend of hers to come forward."

"Radford?"

"Yeah, that's him."

Why were the police looking for Josh Radford? To have put out an appeal on the radio, they must have got something solid on him. How could I find out what it was?

I made a call.

"Jack, sweetheart. It's me."

"Is everything okay?"

"Yeah, fine. I've just been to see Kathy's new shop, and I thought, seeing as I was in West Chipping, that we could grab lunch if you're free."

"That's a great idea. I can get out in about ten minutes. The Gardeners has a nice menu."

"Great, I'll see you there."

"Okay."

"Oh, Jack. Just one more thing. Be a love and find out what Washbridge Police have on Josh Radford, would you? They've apparently just put out an appeal on the radio for anyone who's seen him to come forward."

"You know I can't—"

"Love you. See you in a few minutes."

Chapter 19

"You were right, the food in here is excellent," I said.

Jack and I were in The Gardeners pub, which was doing a roaring lunchtime trade.

"Are you sure you enjoyed it?" He glanced at my plate. "You've left some, which isn't like you."

"It was really nice. It's just that I'm full. I dropped in at Cuppy C earlier and had a muffin." Or two.

He checked his watch. "I'd better be getting back."

"Err, what about—you know?"

"What about *what*?"

"The thing I asked you about."

"I wondered how long it would be before you cracked. That's the real reason you asked me out for lunch, isn't it?"

"Of course not. I don't know how you could even suggest such a thing. I was in West Chipping, and I thought it would be nice for us to have lunch together."

"And it was, but now I have to get back."

"Do I have to beg?"

"Why don't you give it a try?"

"Please, Jack. I just need to know why the police have put out an appeal for anyone who has seen Radford."

He leaned closer. "This is the last time I do this. Understood?"

"Okay. I promise."

"Apparently, they have a number of CCTV sightings of him on the towpath."

"When? Where exactly?"

"That's all I have."

"There must be more to it than that?"

"That's all I know, and it's all you're getting." He leaned over and gave me a kiss. "I'll see you tonight."

"Okay, see you." As I watched him walk away, something suddenly occurred to me. "Hey, Jack. What about the bill?"

He had the audacity to grin just before he disappeared out of the door.

***

Halfway through the afternoon, Mrs V came through to my office and closed the door behind her. For some reason, she was pinching her nose, and pulling a face.

"Is there something the matter, Mrs V?"

"There's a strange man out there." And then in almost a whisper, she added, "He smells like manure."

"What does he want?"

"He says he's from the zoo, and that he needs your help."

"I suppose you'd better show him in."

"Are you sure? He's rather whiffy."

"Yeah. It'll be okay."

"I'll nip down the road and buy some air fresheners while he's in with you."

"Okay."

She hadn't been exaggerating. I could smell him even before he appeared in the doorway. Winky must have done too because he made a beeline for the window.

"I'm out of here. Give me a shout when you've got rid of smelly."

"Thank you for seeing me without an appointment, Mrs

Maxwell." The man offered his hand, but I pretended not to notice.

"No problem. Take a seat, Mr – err – ?"

"Goodroming. Godfrey Goodroming. I'm the head keeper at Candlefield Zoo."

That explained the filthy overalls. I'd been so overpowered by the smell that I hadn't even noticed that the man was a vampire.

"How can I help you, Mr Goodroming?"

"There's something strange going on at the zoo, and I'm hoping you'll be able to get to the bottom of it."

"Strange how?"

"That's just it. I don't really know what's going on. For the last few nights, we've found footprints in the Woolly Massives' enclosure."

"Is someone harming the – err – what did you call them?"

"Woolly Massives. They're like a cross between a wildebeest and an elephant, but way larger. Massive, actually. They don't appear to have been harmed, but it does seem to have put them off their drink."

"Not off their food?"

"No, they're eating normally. They usually have an almost insatiable thirst, but they've barely touched their water since this began."

"I saw one of your employees in my cousins' tea room the other day. She seemed very upset. I'm trying to remember her name. Dab – err?"

"That would be Dabby. She takes care of the Woolly Massives. This business has got her really worried. In fact, it was Dabby who gave me your name. I think your cousins told her about you."

"How can I help?"

"I was hoping you might agree to spend a night at the zoo, to see if you can get to the bottom of what's happening. We've tried posting people at all the entrances overnight, but it hasn't helped."

"Of course. I'll be happy to help if I can. When did you have in mind?"

"Could you come over to the zoo tomorrow night?"

"Sure. No problem."

***

Pixie Petals was located in the Pixie Central area of Candlefield. I had an appointment with Rocky Stone, the head of flower distribution. As always when I visited the pixies, I had to shrink myself in order to get into their offices.

"Welcome to Pixie Petals." The pixie behind reception was wearing a pretty floral pattern dress. "We don't get many non-pixies through those doors." She laughed. "Mainly because they're too big to squeeze through."

"I have an appointment with Mr Stone."

"Which one? We have eight."

"Eight? Really?"

"There's Richard, Ryan, Raymond, Roger, Ronald, Rocky, Ross and Bill."

"Didn't Bill's parents get the memo?"

"Sorry?"

"Never mind. I'm here to see Rocky Stone."

"What's your name, please? I'll let him know you're here."

"Jill Maxwell."

"I think I've heard of you."

"Really?" Once again, my reputation preceded me. Fame could be a little embarrassing sometimes.

"Yes. Didn't you win the Candlefield darts competition last year?"

"Err, no, that wasn't me."

"Are you sure? You're the spitting image of her."

"Positive. If you could just let Mr Stone know I'm here?"

"Of course. Sorry."

The man himself appeared a few minutes later. He was sporting a floral shirt and a kilt. Quite the combination.

"Nice to meet you, Jill." For a pixie, he had an incredibly strong handshake. "Shall we go through to my office?"

He led the way, stopping en route to pick up drinks for us both. The vending machine had a mind-boggling selection of herbal teas, but I stuck with the coffee.

"How is Butter doing?" he asked, once we were seated in his office.

"I think recent events have taken a toll on her."

"I'm not surprised. It must have been stressful enough to have lost her mother, and to have to assume the responsibilities of head of state. I hear she's now using the title of queen—that's a good sign at least."

"How much do you know about the problems they've been experiencing?"

"I'm aware of the crop failure they encountered last season. Normally, we'd have offered to help, but we had a difficult year ourselves. They seem to have pulled through, though."

"Yes, and to try and avoid a repeat of last year's problems, Butter now has three additional plantations."

"Very impressive. We've always had two."

"The thing is, they're experiencing water shortages at all four plantations."

"Really? How can that be? I know Patch well—the guy is first rate. He wouldn't have chosen locations for the new plantations without first ensuring there was a robust water supply."

"He did and there is, but somehow, the reservoirs are regularly running dry."

"How can I help?"

"I don't know that you can, but I told Butter I'd like to speak to her competitors."

"You surely don't think we're in some way responsible, do you?"

"Butter assured me you weren't. She was keen to emphasise the excellent relationship between the two companies. Still, I wouldn't be doing my job if I didn't check every angle."

"Fair enough."

"I guess my main question would be: do you have any idea what might be happening to their water supply?"

"One word: sabotage. I don't see how it can be anything else."

***

The events that had played out at W.O.W. were still buzzing around in my head. I wanted to speak to someone about it, and the only person I could trust not to breathe a word was Aunt Lucy, so while I was in

Candlefield, I dropped in on her.

When I arrived there, she had the vacuum cleaner in pieces.

"Do you know anything about these things, Jill?"

"Not really. I've had some recent experience with a Black Hole Vacuum, but that didn't end well."

"I don't think I've ever heard of those."

"Probably just as well. What seems to be the problem?"

"Lester is the problem!"

"What did he do?"

"I just happened to mention in passing that the suction didn't seem to be as strong as usual, and he took it upon himself to dismantle it, to find out what the problem was. It hasn't worked since."

"Oh dear."

"Men. Don't you sometimes wonder why we bother with them?"

"Definitely. Jack just lumbered me with the bill for lunch."

She stood up and gave the vacuum a kick. "Why don't we have a nice cup of tea? It might take my mind off this piece of junk."

I followed her into the kitchen. "Where's Lily?"

"Fast asleep upstairs." Aunt Lucy pointed to the baby monitor that was clipped to her apron. "I thought I'd take the opportunity to see if I could sort out the vacuum, but I think I'm going to have to buy a new one."

"Couldn't you get it repaired?"

"It's a million years old. It would probably cost as much to get it repaired as it would to buy a new one. You're in luck, Jill, I made a Victoria sponge yesterday."

"Not for me, thanks."

"Aren't you feeling well?"

"I've just had lunch, and I had a muffin at Cuppy C earlier. I couldn't eat another thing."

Once we had our tea and we were seated at the kitchen table, I raised the subject of W.O.W.

"That must have been awkward for you?" Aunt Lucy looked shocked.

"I couldn't believe it; I still can't. It was bad enough to ask me to stab my own grandmother in the back, but to approach me while she was in the same building? The nerve of the woman."

"I assume you turned them down?"

"Of course I did, but I don't know what to do about Grandma. That's why I came over. I wanted to ask your advice."

"I've never had anything to do with W.O.W. Mainly because, as you know, I've spent very little time in the human world. I can't say I've heard of this Belinda Cartwheel, but she must be very brave to risk Grandma's wrath."

"She wasn't so brave when Grandma came back into the hall; she soon shot back to her seat."

"Will you tell your grandmother what happened?"

"I don't know. After the talk, she invited me to join W.O.W, so I thought I might wait until I know more about the organisation, and about Belinda Cartwheel in particular, before I decide what to do."

Just then, there were paw steps on the stairs.

"Someone is on their way to see you." Aunt Lucy grinned. "I don't think he'll want to go for a walk. Lily and I took him to the park not more than twenty minutes ago."

For once, Barry didn't jump up and plant his paws on my chest. There was a good reason for that—balancing precariously on his back was none other than Rhymes, who looked more than a little nervous.

"Will you get me down from here, please, Jill?" The tortoise held out his little arms (are they arms or legs? I'm never sure).

I lifted him off Barry's back, and put him onto the chair next to me.

"Have you managed to get my poems published yet, Jill?"

"It's all in hand. Jack, that's my husband, is in the process of sorting it out."

"You told Jack?" Aunt Lucy looked horrified.

"It's okay. I didn't tell him the poems were by a tortoise. Obviously."

"Phew, thank goodness. I thought for a horrible moment there that—"

"Of course not. I told him the poems were mine."

"What did he make of that?" She grinned.

"I—err—" I glanced across at Rhymes. I couldn't hurt the little guy's feelings by repeating what Jack had actually said. "He thought they were very good."

Aunt Lucy had to put her hand over her mouth to stifle a laugh. Fortunately, Rhymes didn't seem to notice.

"When will my books be ready?" the tortoise asked.

"I'm not sure. In a couple of weeks I would think."

"I'd like to publish a book, too," Barry chipped in.

Oh boy! "I didn't think you could write?"

"I can't, but I'm good at drawing. I could do a picture book. Could you get that published too?"

"I—err—I'm not sure about that."

"Aw, please! You've done it for Rhymes."

"It's only fair, Jill." Aunt Lucy was enjoying this way too much.

"Okay. I'll see what I can do."

Barry was so excited that he jumped up and almost knocked me backwards off the chair.

***

Before going home, I wanted to call in at the office in case there was anything that needed my attention.

"Mrs V, are there any—" I stopped dead in my tracks, horrified by the sight that greeted me.

A man was standing behind Mrs V. He had one arm around her waist, and was brandishing a knife in his other hand. It was Josh Radford; he had the same plaster on his chin, and an insane look in his eyes.

"Don't come any closer or I'll cut her!" He yelled.

"Let her go!"

"No! Stay where you are, or she gets it."

"Don't be stupid, Josh. We can talk about this."

"The police think I murdered Pam. Did you tell them I did it?"

"No, of course not. I have no evidence to say you did, and besides, the police aren't interested in anything I might have to say."

At the same time as I was talking to him, I was trying to figure out the best spell to use to rescue Mrs V.

"Why do they think I did it, then? I never murdered anyone."

"I believe they have CCTV of you on the towpath. Why were you down there?"

"I didn't kill Pam. I would never have hurt her."

"Why were you there, then?"

"I was short of cash, so I robbed a couple of boats. That's all. I didn't kill anyone."

Only then, did I remember what Suki Coates had said about the burglar's face piercing. The plaster on Radford's chin could easily have been covering the injury caused when the stud was ripped out.

"I believe you, but doing this isn't going to help your case. Why don't you put that knife down, and we can talk?"

"I'm done talking. You're supposed to be a private investigator, aren't you? I need you to find out who the murderer was, and to tell the police I didn't do it."

Just then, a jet of water hit him square in the eye; the shock caused him to stumble backwards. That was my opportunity. After casting the 'power' spell, I knocked him to the ground and kicked the knife away.

"Mrs V. Go through to my office and call the police."

Apparently unaffected by her ordeal, she hurried next door. While she was gone, I used magic to bind Radford.

"They're on their way," Mrs V said. "Where did you get that rope from?"

"I—err, never mind that. How did you manage to spray him with water?"

"Luckily, I'd decided to test drive some of the new clown props I bought yesterday. The up-sleeve water pistol turned out to be a wise investment."

Chapter 20

"Do you think Mrs V will be in work today?" Jack said over breakfast. "She must be pretty shaken up after what happened yesterday."

"She sounded fine when I phoned her last night. She may look like a fragile old lady, but underneath, she's as tough as they come. I told her to stay off for as long as she wanted, but she insisted she'd be in this morning."

"I hope you appreciate her. That woman is a one-off. I still can't believe she managed to foil Radford with a water pistol."

"Not any old water pistol. An up-sleeve water pistol."

"Whatever it was. She certainly wasn't *clowning* around." He laughed at his own joke. "Get it? Clowning around?"

"Whatever you do, don't give up the day job for a career in stand-up."

"I still don't understand why Radford went to your office. Why didn't he just do a runner and get as far away as possible?"

"That's been bothering me too. Just before Mrs V squirted him with water, he was still insisting he was innocent. He even said he wanted me to find the real murderer. It doesn't make sense."

***

When I arrived at the office, there she was, knitting clown socks, as though nothing had happened.

"Are you sure you're okay to be here, Mrs V? You could have taken the rest of the week off."

"It'll take more than that silly young man to stop me coming to work. And besides, I have lots of clown socks to knit. Are you sure you wouldn't like some, Jill?"

"I'm positive. By the way, I've ordered a new desk, which should be delivered today. It's for the new office manager."

"Will he be based in your office or out here?"

"It'd probably be best if he shared your office. He might find Winky too much of a distraction. I thought he could sit over there by the window if that's okay by you?"

"That's fine by me, dear. Do you think he'd like any clown socks?"

"I'm not sure. It might be best to let him settle in before you ask him that."

"As you wish."

All morning, I'd been mentally preparing myself to endure Winky's presentation. It was my own stupid fault for having given him a non-existent job in the first place. No matter how boring it was, I'd have to make sure I didn't nod off halfway through or I'd be in the cat house forever more.

When I walked into my office, much to my surprise, there was no sign of the whiteboards. Winky didn't even acknowledge me; he was far too busy sunning himself in the window sill.

"I'm ready for your presentation."

He turned to face me, but said nothing. Instead, he pointed to a small white envelope on my desk.

"What's that?"

"You'd better read it."

I ripped it open. "You're resigning?"

"You left me no choice. My time and skillset are too valuable to waste on someone who isn't one-hundred per cent committed to improving their business."

"But, I—"

"Don't waste your breath. My mind is made up."

I had to be careful that I didn't show the relief I felt. Instead, I put on a really disappointed face. "I'm sorry you feel like that."

"I do. What's the point in wasting my energy on you when I could channel it into my own business ventures?"

"Fair enough. I guess I brought it on myself. What about the office manager? Will you be okay when he starts here next week?"

"I pity the poor man. You're unmanageable."

"I wouldn't say—"

"I've said my piece. There's no point in wasting any more time on it." He hesitated. "How's the old bag lady, by the way?"

"She's okay. Did you see what happened yesterday?"

"Of course I did. I was just on my way out to tackle that yob when she decked him with the water pistol."

"That's really sweet of you. Mrs V will be thrilled to hear that you were so concerned."

"Like she'd ever believe that."

***

I was surprised to find that the owner of Always Flowers was a burly werewolf by the name of Artemis Reed.

In contrast to the warm welcome I'd received from Pixie Petals, Reed had been very reluctant to meet with me.

Only after much cajoling had he agreed to spare me a few minutes of his time.

Always Flowers were located on a rundown industrial estate at the far reaches of Candlefield. The building was practically anonymous, with only a small name plaque next to the front door.

"You're going to have to make this quick," Reed said, once he'd taken me through to his office. "I'm a busy man."

"That's okay. I'll keep it brief. As I mentioned on the phone, I'm working for Queen Buttercup."

"Oh, la-di-da. You mean Butter, don't you?"

"Yeah. I'm not sure if you're aware of this, but the floral fairies have experienced water shortages that have caused crop failures."

"Of course I'm aware of it. I make it my business to know what's happening with my competitors. What I don't understand is why you think I'd care."

What a piece of work this guy was.

"I've already spoken to Pixie Petals, and I was hoping to—"

"Look, lady, I get it. You think we had something to do with it, but we didn't. I have much better things to do with my time than worry about the Florals or Petals, both of whom will be out of business in a few years."

"What do you mean by that?"

"It really isn't rocket science. The days of real flowers are numbered. Why should people continue to buy them when they could have something that is practically indistinguishable, and which will last forever? I don't need to sabotage the competition; they'll go out of business soon enough anyway."

"Surely, the two business models can exist side by side? Real and artificial — there must be a market for both?"

"We'll see." He tapped his watch. "Your time is up."

I wasn't sure what to make of that. Reed was an obnoxious man, but I couldn't convince myself he was behind the sabotage of the water supplies. Rightly or wrongly, he seemed confident that he was already on his way to dominating the market, and had no need to resort to those kinds of tactics.

It seemed that I was back to square one.

***

Back at the office, Winky was still flashing disappointed looks my way. Ridiculously, even though I'd initially been elated at his shock resignation, I was now feeling bad at the amount of work he'd put into the project.

"Would you like some salmon?"

"Guilty conscience?"

"No, I just thought you might be hungry."

"You don't usually offer. Most days, I have to beg you to feed me."

"That's not true." I opened a tin and put the salmon into his bowl. "How long are you going to guilt-trip me for?"

"A month or two should do it."

Great!

When she came through to my office, Mrs V almost tripped over her knitting.

"Be careful, Mrs V. I thought you were knitting clown socks?"

"I am."

"That's very long. It looks more like a scarf."

"It's for Rhubarb. He's a stilt-walking clown, so he needs extra-long socks."

"I see."

"There's a young woman here to see you. Her name is Kirsty, but she won't give her last name. She says you left your business card with her."

"Oh?" I didn't recall a Kirsty. "I suppose you'd better show her in."

As soon as the young woman walked through the door, I remembered her; she'd been working behind the bar at Liberty's when I was looking for Duncan.

"Hi. Take a seat."

"No, I'm not staying." She fidgeted from one foot to the other. "I wasn't sure if I should come to see you or not."

"Is something wrong?"

"I've been debating whether or not to contact you ever since you came into the bar. I nearly phoned you a few times, but changed my mind. I hadn't intended coming here today, but I was in town shopping when I realised your offices were just around the corner. I probably shouldn't have come."

"You're here now, so you might as well tell me what you came here to say."

"I couldn't talk when you came into the bar because we were busy. Otherwise I might have said something then."

"About?"

"Duncan."

I'd tried to contact Duncan in connection with the Pam Turton case, but now Radford had been arrested, there seemed to be no point in talking to him.

"Did you give him my card? He never contacted me."

"No, I didn't. That's why I'm here. To warn you to stay away from him. The man's a psycho."

"What makes you say that?"

"I've seen it at first hand. He's very charming when you first meet him. When he came to work at the bar, I kind of fell for him. After a couple of weeks, he asked me out on a date. It seemed to go okay until we bumped into an ex of mine. Kev and I are still friends, so I stopped for a chat with him. Duncan went crazy and started acting like a madman. He hit Kev and then turned on me. I reckon he would have hit me too if some passers-by hadn't intervened."

"Didn't either you or your ex report it to the police?"

"No, we probably should have. The thing is, the next time I saw Duncan at work, he was all sweetness and light. It was as if nothing had happened. But I can't get that other side of him out of my mind. When you came around asking about him, I didn't give him your card in case he did the same thing to you. That's why I'm here now — to warn you to stay away from him."

"Right, thanks. I really do appreciate you taking the time to do this."

With Radford's arrest, I had thought the Pam Turton case was closed, but now I was beginning to have second thoughts. Radford was a thief, and what he'd done to Mrs V was unforgiveable. But had he murdered Pam?

Despite Kirsty's warning, I thought maybe I would pay Duncan a visit.

Chapter 21

It was almost eleven o'clock, and Jack was getting ready to go to bed.

"What exactly is it you'll be doing at the zoo?" he said.

"I don't really know. Just looking out for intruders, I guess. The zookeepers found footprints in the Woolly Massives' enclosure."

"Those animals sound dangerous. Will you be safe?"

"I'll be fine. From all accounts, they're just big softies. I should warn you, though, I'll probably stink when I get back. Mrs V had to buy a bagful of air fresheners after the head zookeeper had been to see me at the office."

"That's okay. You can sleep outside until the smell has worn off."

"Thanks, buddy."

After changing into some old clothes, which I'd be happy to throw away after this particular case was over, I magicked myself over to Candlefield Zoo. I'd arranged to meet Godfrey Goodroming at the gates of the zoo, which had now closed for the day.

Standing next to him was the young woman who'd been in such distress in Cuppy C.

"Thanks for coming, Jill." Godfrey greeted me. "I think you've already met Dabby."

"Not met, exactly." I turned to her. "But I did see you with Pearl."

"I'm sorry about making such a show of myself. It's been so upsetting."

"Don't worry about it. Do you think that maybe these intruders, whoever they are, have spooked the creatures and put them off their drink?"

"I suppose it's possible; I hadn't really considered that. I was just saying to Godfrey that I'd be happy to stay here with you tonight if that would help?"

"Thanks for the offer, Dabby, but I work best alone. If you could just show me to the enclosure, that would be great."

I'd expected the Woolly Massives to be large, but nothing could have prepared me for the sheer enormity of the creatures.

"Are you sure they aren't dangerous?" I hesitated at the gate to their enclosure.

"They're perfectly safe." Dabby reassured me. "They look scary, but they're really just big softies. Aren't you, Maisy?" She held out a hand to the nearest of the animals.

Maisy came over and licked Dabby's hand with her enormous tongue.

Having seen that, I felt confident enough to enter the enclosure, and close the gate behind me.

"Where were the footprints seen?"

"Near their water trough. I'll show you."

Dabby led the way across the huge, muddy enclosure — thank goodness I'd had the foresight to wear wellingtons.

"All around here." She pointed. "You can't see them now because the Woollies have trampled all over this area."

"Did it appear to be more than one person?"

"It's difficult to be sure, but I'd say probably not."

"What's in the lake?"

"That isn't a lake." She smiled. "That's the Woollies' water trough. They *really* like their water. Usually, anyway."

"Okay, thanks. You can leave me to it now. Just one final thing, what are the other two called?"

"That's Mabel and the one over there is Malcolm."

"Maisy, Mabel and Malcolm. Right. Got it."

"I'll see you in the morning, Jill."

"Goodnight."

***

This was becoming a bit of a habit, and frankly, one I could have done without. First, I get the job of spending the night at Washbridge House to guard the flowerbeds, and now I had to spend tonight knee deep in mud at the zoo, keeping watch over the Woolly Massives. I'd failed miserably to stop the flower thefts, but there was no way anyone was going to walk off with one of these huge beasts without my noticing it.

The truth was, I had no idea what the intruder or intruders were up to. There was nothing of any value in the enclosure for them to steal, and if they'd meant the Woollies harm, they'd had plenty of opportunity to do that already.

After a couple of cold muddy hours, I began to relax around the large creatures. It was obvious that I held no interest for them, and for the most part they kept their distance. As with my stint at Washbridge House, the biggest challenge was staying awake. The best way to do that would be to keep my mind active, so I set myself the task of coming up with an interest that Jack and I could share. His recent suggestions had left me cold. Working out together at the gym sounded like hard work, and I certainly didn't want to join the clown school. I needed something that I could buy into one-hundred per cent. Something that I wouldn't get bored with easily.

I can hear you at the back, shouting custard creams and blueberry muffins.

In order to keep warm, I took a walk around the enclosure, doing my best to pick out the least muddy areas. As I walked past the enormous water trough, I stopped dead in my tracks because right there in front of me was a fresh set of footprints. And they definitely weren't mine.

I looked all around, but could see no sign of the intruder. By now, I was pretty sure that there was only one of them, but where were they hiding? Was it a witch or a wizard using the 'invisible' spell? I didn't think so because I would have sensed their presence. How had I missed them? I was usually so observant.

Oh no!

Now I seemed to be missing one of the Woolly Massives.

Mabel and Maisy were over the other side of the water trough, but where was Malcolm? This could not be happening. If I couldn't keep track of something the size of several double-decker buses, my reputation as a P.I. would be in tatters.

I ran around the enclosure like some kind of idiot, in the vain hope that Malcolm might be hiding somewhere. As if that was possible.

Exhausted, I leaned against a tree and tried to get my breath, but as I did, Mabel disappeared right in front of my eyes. This time, though, I'd actually seen the Woolly Massive vanish, and I was in no doubt that magic was involved. Who was behind it, and what had they done with the two missing creatures? There was only one way to find out.

"Maisy, come here, girl," I called to the remaining animal.

She hesitated, probably more than a little freaked out at having lost her two companions.

I edged my way closer, and tried again.

"Come on, Maisy. It's okay."

Much to my relief, she ambled over to me. And not a moment too soon because I'd no sooner grabbed hold of her thick woolly coat than both she and I were transported out of the enclosure.

The next thing I knew, we were standing beside a large body of water from which Malcolm and Mabel had already started to slake their enormous thirst.

"Come on, girl. Drink up." The male voice belonged to someone standing on the other side of Maisy.

I let go of the Woolly's coat, and dropped to my feet. "What's your game?"

The wizard almost jumped out of his skin when I stepped out from behind Maisy. "Who are you?"

"You don't get to ask the questions!" I snapped. "You have ten seconds before I turn you into a slug."

"I'm not scared of you." His nervous laugh said otherwise.

"Nine, eight, seven."

"Wait! Aren't you? You are, aren't you?"

"Six, five, four."

"Okay, okay. Stop!"

"Start talking, and it had better be good."

"I was paid to bring the animals here. I'm just a hired-hand. I don't harm them, and I always take them back afterwards."

"Where is *here* anyway?" I took a good look around, and suddenly the penny dropped. "This is the floral fairies' plantation, isn't it?"

"One of them, yes. I take the animals to each one in turn before taking them back to the zoo. I would never have agreed to take this job if it had involved hurting these creatures."

"Who hired you to do this?"

"They'll kill me if they know I told you."

"That's a chance you're going to have to take. It's either that or life as a slug."

"Okay, okay. I'll tell you."

And he did.

***

Godfrey and Dabby returned at the crack of dawn.

"Did the intruders come back?" he asked, as they joined me in the enclosure.

"Are the Woollies alright?" Dabby glanced at her charges.

"The animals are all fine, and yes, the intruder did come back, but he won't be bothering you again."

"Did you hand him over to the police?" Godfrey said.

"Let's just say that the person responsible for this outrageous act will be brought to justice." I turned to Dabby. "And I'm confident the Woollies will start drinking normally again now."

"I hope so. Was it the intruder that had upset them? Is that why they weren't drinking?"

"Something like that."

This time when I magicked myself back home, I remembered not to land inside the house. I was muddy and very smelly. The Woollies were perfectly lovely creatures, but boy, did they pong.

My clothes were so smelly that there was no way I'd ever be able to wear any of them again. At least I'd had the good sense to change into old ones before going to the zoo.

It was just turned midnight, and pitch black. There was no chance anyone would see me, so I took off all my clothes and threw them in the bin. I'd no sooner done that than a bright light illuminated the whole of the backyard. It was so bright that it took me a few seconds to work out where it was coming from.

Our new neighbours, the Livelys, had had a security light fitted, and I'd just triggered it.

Oh bum!

At that moment, I saw the curtains twitch in next-door's back bedroom. Britt and Kit must have been woken by the light, and were no doubt about to check what had triggered it. If I wasn't quick, they'd see me standing there, stark naked. There wasn't time to dash around the side of the house, so I had to quickly cast the 'invisible' spell.

Phew, just in time.

When I climbed into bed, Jack said, "What's that light?"
"The new neighbours have had a security light fitted."
"What triggered it?"
"I don't know. Probably just their cat."

Chapter 22

The next morning, Jack was kind enough to offer to get up first and make breakfast.

What? Of course I hadn't cast a spell to make him do it.

"Thank you for making breakfast for me, sweetheart." I treated him to a sexy smile.

"Is there something you'd like to tell me, Jill?" He was seated at the kitchen table, and something told me he wasn't a happy bunny.

"Look, I got mixed up about whose turn it was to make breakfast. It was a genuine mistake."

"I'm not talking about breakfast."

"What then?"

"I took the rubbish out to the bin a few minutes ago, and—"

"I know those old clothes reek, but what else was I supposed to do with them?"

"I'm not talking about your stinky clothes. While I was out there, I saw Britt, and you'll never guess what she said to me?"

"Was it: I've forgotten your name again?"

"No."

"I know what she said. It was how did you land yourself a wife like Jill, wasn't it?"

"Actually, she asked how long you and I had been naturists."

Oh bum! I must not have been quick enough with the 'invisible' spell.

"What a very strange thing to say."

"That's what I thought too until she told me that she'd seen you standing next to the dustbin last night. Stark naked."

"Did you tell her she must have been mistaken?"

"She saw you, Jill."

"You should have tried to persuade her that she was dreaming. It was all your fault anyway!"

"What?" He laughed. "How was it my fault that you were standing in the backyard naked?"

"Because the last time I came home covered in mud, you had a go at me. What did you say to her?"

"I explained to her that *we* weren't naturists."

"Thank goodness for that."

"I told her that it was *just you* who was." And with that, he grabbed his jacket. "Sorry, I have to dash."

He was kidding. He was definitely kidding. That guy could be such a joker at times.

***

I was just about to get into the car when someone called my name.

It was Britt.

"Hi, err — ?"

"Jill."

"Have you got a minute?"

"I was just on my way to work."

"It won't take long."

"Okay." I went over to join her.

"I just wanted to say that I think you're very brave."

"Oh?"

"To have the confidence to do what you do."

"Wait a minute. I wouldn't want you to get the wrong idea."

"It's okay. Jack has explained. I think that makes you even braver. To do it alone, I mean."

"I think you may have got the wrong end of the stick."

"There's no need to wait until after dark. It won't embarrass Kit or me if you want to go naked in the back garden during daylight hours."

"Jack was just pulling your leg. I'm not really a naturist."

"Oh? Then, why were you—"

"I'd been working on a case, and I came home covered in mud. My clothes were smelly too, so I didn't want to walk into the house wearing them. Of course, if I'd realised you'd had a security light installed, I would never have—you know."

"I see. I hope I haven't embarrassed you. It's just that Jack said—"

"It's okay. Don't worry about it. I'll be having a few choice words with him later."

That man was so dead.

When I arrived at the office building, Mrs V was standing at the top of the stairs, signing paperwork for a man at her side.

"Who was that?" I asked when I joined her.

"They've just delivered the new desk."

"Great." I reached for the door handle, but Mrs V grabbed my arm.

"What exactly did you order, Jill?"

"Just a regular desk. I ordered it online. I got a great discount too: Eighty-five per cent off."

"Did you happen to notice the colour when you placed the order?"

"No. I assumed it would just be desk coloured."

"Right." She let go of my arm.

"Orange?"

"At least the chair matches," she said. "You should take a look at the drawers."

I walked over to the orange monstrosity. "What are these?"

"I think they're dolphins."

"Why are there pictures of dolphins on the drawers?"

"Or they might be porpoises." I got the distinct impression that Mrs V was enjoying this. "The paperwork says it's a limited edition desk." She passed me the delivery note. "Perhaps the new office manager will like dolphins." She finally lost it, and dissolved into laughter.

I, though, was not amused.

"Nice desk." Winky grinned.

"Shut it!"

"You should get rid of that old thing of yours and get one just like it. Orange would go really well in here."

While I was formulating a witty rejoinder, the grin suddenly disappeared from his face and he shot under the sofa. Moments later, the temperature dropped several degrees, no doubt heralding a ghostly visit. Could it be the colonel and Priscilla? I hadn't seen those two for some time.

It wasn't.

"Hi, Jill." My mother was all smiles.

"Hello, darling." So too was my father.

"You two look like a couple of Cheshire cats. What are you so happy about?"

"We have some really big news." She was clearly

bursting to tell me.

"First, though," my father jumped in. "We owe you an apology."

"Oh?"

"Your mother and I now realise that the whole anniversary party was a bad idea."

"You think so?"

"We didn't mean to upset anyone," Mum said. "We thought they'd all enjoy a good party."

"And you'd get lots of presents."

Ignoring the jibe, she continued, "Anyway, we'd like to apologise for putting you in such a difficult position."

"It wasn't fair of us," Dad said.

"It's not me who you should be apologising to. It was a horrible thing to do to Alberto and Blodwyn."

"We realise that now, don't we, Darlene?"

"That's still no excuse for bringing their exes to the party." My mother clearly wasn't as forgiving as my father. "I was so embarrassed."

"We've apologised to them both, haven't we, Darlene?"

"Hmm."

Something told me that my mother's apology had been less than sincere.

"So, are we forgiven?" Dad said.

"If Alberto and Blodwyn are willing to forgive and forget, I see no reason not to do the same. And you'll no doubt be returning all the gifts?"

"That would just be rude," Mum said. "And besides, not *everyone* bought us a present."

If she thought that sly dig was going to make me feel guilty, she was sadly mistaken.

"Okay. What's your big news?"

"You'll never guess. Go on try." Mum teased.

"We're buying Spooky Wooky," Dad blurted out.

Mum scowled at him for stealing her thunder.

"Really?" I hadn't seen that coming. "Are Harry and Larry selling up?"

"Yes, they've decided to buy a small bungalow at the seaside."

"You two don't know anything about running a tea room, do you?"

"How difficult can it be?" Mum waved away my concerns. "It's only tea and cakes."

"What do Alberto and Blodwyn have to say about all this?"

"They're just as excited as we are," Dad said. "The four of us will be running it together."

"Say you're pleased for us, Jill," Mum said.

"Of course I am."

"We're going to change the name too."

"Why? I like Spooky Wooky. It's a great name."

"New owners, new name," Mum said. "Would you like to hear it?"

"Sure."

"Cakey C."

"You can't use that."

"Why not?"

"You've blatantly stolen the idea from the twins' shop, Cuppy C."

"I wouldn't say *stolen*. It's more of a homage."

"I'm not sure the twins would agree."

"Why should they care? It's not like we're even in the same world, is it?"

"I suppose not. The twins give me family discount. Will

you do the same?"

"Of course, darling," Dad said.

"Not so quick, Josh," Mum jumped in. "How much discount do they give you?"

"Fifty per cent," I lied.

"I very much doubt that. You can have twenty."

Drat! Foiled again. "When do you take over?"

"Larry and Harry wanted a quick sale, so with a bit of luck, we should be up and running within a couple of weeks. The shop closes today to allow us to do some minor refurbishments."

"That quick? Wow! What about things like learning how to make all the different coffees? Have you factored in time for training?"

"How difficult can it be?" Mum shrugged.

"It took me ages, and I still wasn't very good at it."

"Yes, well, it's horses for courses. I'm sure you're a perfectly good P.I."

"Gee, thanks."

"We'll obviously be having a big re-launch party. Everyone who's anyone will be invited. You can come too."

"Thanks, Mum."

"Do you think Madeline will come to the relaunch?" Dad said.

"I'm not sure. If you tell me when you have the date finalised, I'll let her know."

"Your parents are creepy," Winky said when he emerged from under the sofa.

"They're ghosts, what do you expect?"

"I don't mean that. Don't they have new partners now?"

"Yeah. Alberto and Blodwyn."

"So why do those two spend so much time together? It's weird if you ask me."

The cat had a point.

***

I was due to teach at CASS later today, but first I wanted to pay a visit to Butter.

As soon as I saw her, I could tell that the stress of recent events had taken its toll.

"You were very mysterious on the phone, Jill."

"I thought this would be best done face to face."

"Not more bad news, I hope. I'm not sure I can handle any more."

"A mix of good and bad. I'll give you the good news first if I may?"

"Please do. I could do with some."

"I know what has been causing your water shortages, and I'm confident that the situation has now been resolved."

Her face lit up. "Are you sure? That would be fantastic if it's true."

"As you and Patch suspected, it was sabotage, but of the strangest kind."

I went on to tell her about the Woolly Massives and their insatiable thirst.

"Let me see if I've got this straight." She scratched her chin. "Are you saying that these creatures were magicked from the zoo to our plantations, so that they could empty our reservoirs?"

"That's right. I would probably never have got to the

bottom of it had the zookeeper not become so concerned that the creatures had lost their appetite for water."

"What about the animals? Are they okay?"

"They're perfectly fine. There was never any intention to do them harm. The objective was to bring your business to its knees."

"And they almost succeeded. But who would do something like this?"

"That brings me to the bad news that I mentioned. The actual act of magicking the creatures to your plantations was carried out by a wizard, but he was only doing it for the money."

"Who was paying him? Was it Artemis Reed? I never did trust that man."

"Reed is a nasty piece of work, but he wasn't responsible for this. I'm sorry to have to tell you that the person behind this is your sister."

"Tulip?"

"I'm afraid so."

Obviously shocked by the revelation, Butter had to take a seat. "Are you certain about this, Jill?"

"I only have the word of the wizard who carried out the sabotage, but I have to tell you, I found him credible."

"I knew she was unhappy with some of the changes I've been forced to make, but I never thought she'd do anything like this."

"It's always possible I'm wrong."

"I sincerely hope you are, but either way, I intend to get to the bottom of this." Butter got back to her feet. "It seems that once again I'm in your debt. I do hope that some day I'll be able to repay you."

"Paying my bill will be thanks enough."

"Let me have it as soon as you can, and I'll ensure it's paid immediately. Along with a nice bonus."

Music to my ears.

Chapter 23

Reggie was waiting for me at the airship hangar. By the look of it, we'd be the only two travelling this morning. When he spotted me, he managed a half-hearted smile, and it was obvious that something was wrong.

"Are you okay, Reggie?"

"He's threatened to fire me."

"The headmaster?"

"Yeah, yesterday morning just before I left for home. He says my timekeeping is terrible, and that my work isn't up to standard. I admit I've been a couple of minutes late on a few occasions, but I always make up the time at the end of each day. And there's never been any complaint about my work before as far as I'm aware. Unless people have been going behind my back."

"I don't think anyone would do that. They'd come to you first, wouldn't they?"

"That's what I said. I asked him who'd been complaining, but he wouldn't name names."

"Wouldn't or couldn't? I shouldn't worry about it. You're much too valuable to that school for him to let you go."

"I doubt that. He's already allowed teachers who have years of experience to walk away. If you ask me, he's only interested in bringing in his own people. Three new teachers started on Monday, and I can tell you this, Jill. They're not CASS people. And it isn't only me who thinks that way."

"If I get a chance to speak to him today, I'll put in a good word for you."

"Thanks, I appreciate that, but I'm not sure it will do

any good."

Reggie was very quiet on the journey over, clearly lost in his own thoughts. CASS was his life; he'd be devastated if that was taken away from him. The more I heard about Maligarth, the less I liked the sound of him.

I was disappointed that the low cloud meant I was unable to see Sybil's nest as we passed over the White Mountains, but a few minutes later, we touched down on the playing field.

"Keep your chin up," I said, as Reggie and I parted ways.

"I'll do my best."

If I'd expected the atmosphere in the staffroom to be more uplifting, I was to be sorely disappointed. When Reggie had visited my offices the previous week, he'd mentioned that Philomena Eastwest had taken early retirement. Judging by the long faces on some of those still there, she might not be the only one to leave.

"Morning everyone." I tried to sound as bright and breezy as possible.

My cheery greeting was met only with a series of grunts and sour faces, so I decided to get myself a coffee; I was going to need something to get me through the day.

"I told you, didn't I?" Natasha Fastjersey, the head librarian, had crept up behind me, and almost caused me to spill my drink. "I told you the headmistress was leaving."

"You did. It's such a pity. Desdemona Nightowl has done such wonderful work here. What do you make of the new headmaster?"

She gestured to the two men seated in the corner of the room, who I hadn't noticed until then. In a hushed voice, she said, "I probably shouldn't say. Things have a habit of getting back to *his highness*."

Reggie had mentioned that the new headmaster had brought in a number of new teachers, so I made my excuses to Natasha, and made my way over to the newcomers.

"Hi, I'm Jill Maxwell." I took the seat opposite them.

"Hello." The taller of the two said, somewhat begrudgingly.

The other man could only manage a nod before going back to his book.

"I take it you're both new here?" I didn't intend to let them off the hook that easily. "Where did you teach before?"

The silent man pretended to check his watch, and then stood up. "I have to be somewhere else."

"So do I." Moustache followed him out of the door.

The change of atmosphere in the room was almost immediate.

I turned to the others. "Do I have B.O. or something?"

"Well done, Jill." Carmel Roundcake grinned. "Those two are poison."

"I assume they're the headmaster's new recruits?"

"Two of them. There are three so far."

"*So far?*"

"He won't be satisfied until he's got rid of all the old guard," Desmond Crawfish chipped in.

"You mustn't let him drive you out. You have to resist him."

"Easier said than done," Hattie Kindred said. "You

haven't heard the half of it, Jill."

"Tell me, then."

"The man is rewriting our lessons. That's totally unacceptable to me."

"Tell her about the forbidden spells," Desmond urged.

"What are they?" I was intrigued.

Hattie glanced at the door, to make sure the newcomers hadn't returned. "There are some spells that are considered too dangerous for general use; that's why they were banned many years ago. The new headmaster insists that no magic should be out of bounds, and is pushing for them to be added to the curriculum."

"Can he do that?"

"Who's going to stop him?"

"If everyone refuses to teach the forbidden spells, then—"

"Then he'll just bring in someone else who will. You've just met two of them."

"I've had enough of this place," Carmel said. "He'll have my resignation at the end of the month."

"You can't do that. What about the kids?"

"I'm sorry, Jill. If I thought my staying would make a difference, then I would. I'm not the only one who'll be leaving. I know of at least two others."

"How did things come to this?" I said. "How did Maligarth get appointed? And who is he, anyway?"

"That's something we'd all like to know."

***

Despite my misgivings about the new headmaster, I still had a class to teach. If I could have chosen, I would have preferred to be facing the first years. Instead, I had the challenge of class five-gamma who would soon be graduating and leaving CASS. This bunch had none of the reserve of the younger pupils. If they had something on their minds, I could rely on them to let me know.

"You were rubbish in the Elite Competition, Miss!" Bobby Greenside shouted before I'd even had chance to greet the class.

"Good morning to you, too, Bobby."

"Why did you throw it away like that?"

"I'm sure you'll have read the articles in the press."

"We saw the whole thing on TV," Carl Bestwick said.

"How did you manage that? I didn't think you were allowed to watch TV during term time."

"Someone smuggled a DVD in."

"In that case, you'll have seen what happened."

"But it was only a stupid dragon, Miss," Bobby said. "You should have left it to fight its own battles."

"I happen to know that particular dragon. Her name is Sybil if you're interested. She has the cutest little baby called Cora."

"Aww," Veronica Reedmore cooed. "I think you did the right thing, Miss."

"Thank you, Veronica. Now, we really should —"

"Do you think you'll ever make it to level six, Miss?" Bobby wasn't done yet.

Before I could respond, Lucas Kingston jumped in, "What does it matter what level she is? Everyone knows that Miss is the most powerful witch in Candlefield."

"My dad says Ma Chivers is," Bobby shot back.

"Your dad is stupid. Like you."

The rest of the class began to laugh and goad Bobby, but it didn't last long because moments later, the door opened, and the room fell silent.

"I do apologise for the interruption," said the man standing in the doorway. "When I heard all that noise, I assumed the class must be unattended."

"I'm sorry about the noise."

"I'm Mr Maligarth, the new head. You must be Mrs Maxwell."

"That's right."

"I had intended to send you a note to ask if you'd come to my office after you'd finished your lesson."

"Yes, of course."

"Excellent. Carry on."

"It sounds like you're in trouble, Miss," Bobby quipped.

I was too shocked to respond. I'd fully expected to meet the new headmaster today, but I hadn't anticipated that he would turn out to be the same man who had invaded my dreams only a few weeks earlier.

Despite being unnerved by my run-in with the headmaster, I still had a lesson to give. This week, the kids had elected to discuss sport in the human world. That had caused a number of arguments: primarily whether or not sup sports were better than human sports. Some of the children insisted that BoundBall was far superior to anything to be found in the human world. Others insisted that football was way better. I stayed pretty much on the sideline during that particular debate because I didn't have much time for sport—human or sup. Thankfully, by the time the debate moved onto which was the best football team, the bell rang to end the lesson.

"Good luck with the headmaster." Bobby grinned. "I hope you don't get the sack."

The last time I'd been to this office was when Desdemona Nightowl had shown me the room of shadows, which was deep below the school. There, she'd entrusted me with the secret code that was used to access the Core.

"Mrs Maxwell, do come in." The headmaster's smile didn't reach his eyes.

"Please call me Jill."

"I'd prefer to stick with Mrs Maxwell. I don't hold with some of the informalities that my predecessor encouraged."

"As you wish."

"Do take a seat." He walked behind his desk, which along with most of the other furniture in the room, had been changed since my last visit. Everything was now black, including the new carpet and curtains.

"I like what you've done in here," I lied.

"Thank you. Obviously, I was already familiar with your name before I joined the school, having read about your many *exploits.*"

There was something about the way he said the word exploits that left me in no doubt he didn't approve.

"I try to keep a low profile, but it isn't always possible."

"Hmm. It's my understanding that you teach the pupils some kind of human studies?"

"I'm not sure I'd describe it as human studies. I simply give them an insight into what it's like to live in the human world."

"Personally, I'm not convinced that encouraging our

young people to align themselves with humans is a good thing."

"That's not how I'd describe what I do. Basically, I'm just making sure that those who elect to venture into the human world are better prepared."

"We may have to revisit that at a future date because there's something more important I'd like to discuss with you today."

"Oh?" I had a horrible feeling I knew exactly what that *something* was.

"It's long been a tradition of this school that the outgoing head leaves certain — err —" He hesitated, clearly searching for the right word. "*Sensitive* information for their successor. Unfortunately, for reasons I don't fully understand, Ms Nightowl failed to do that."

"Just an oversight, surely. Have you contacted her?"

"I've tried, but the *woman* seems to have disappeared."

"I'm sure she'll turn up soon. Maybe she's just taking a well-deserved break."

"I'd like to show you something, Mrs Maxwell." He made his way over to the bookcase — one of the few items of furniture which had not been replaced.

Without a moment's hesitation, he pressed the spine of the book titled: The Myth and Magic Yearbook, causing the bookcase to slide to one side.

"You don't look surprised, Mrs Maxwell. I take it you've seen this passageway before?"

"Err, no." Even I didn't think I sounded very convincing.

"Really? Maybe you'd care to follow me."

He led the way along the narrow passageway, and down the spiral staircase.

"This is the room of shadows." His eyes seemed to be burning into me. "But I'm sure you already know that."

"I've never seen this room before. Until now, the only secret passageway I was aware of was the one I used when I first visited CASS."

"You see, Mrs Maxwell, I refuse to believe that Ms Nightowl would have abandoned the school without first passing on the secrets she knew about this room."

"You surely don't think she told me?"

When he started to walk towards me, I had a sudden flashback to the nightmare that had invaded my sleep only a few weeks earlier.

His eyes were now glowing orange, and I could feel a pressure building inside my head. I edged away from him until my back was against the plinth.

"Give me the code!"

The pressure was becoming unbearable. I had to act quickly, so I cast the 'power' spell, and used every ounce of my focus and strength to push him back.

"I'm sorry, but I have no idea what you're talking about, Headmaster. This is the first time I've ever seen this room."

He was clearly shaken by the force of the spell I'd used to repel him. "Very well, Mrs Maxwell. My mistake."

I hurried past him, and made my way back to his office.

By the time he'd closed the bookcase, he seemed to have recomposed himself. "Thank you for coming to see me, Mrs Maxwell. I've enjoyed our little chat. I have a feeling we'll be seeing much more of one another in the future."

Normally, before leaving CASS, I called into the staffroom, but today, I couldn't wait to get away from that place. I was sure of one thing: the headmistress had been right not to entrust Maligarth with the code to the Core. The man positively oozed evil.

After the incident in the room of shadows, my initial reaction had been to tender my resignation and walk away for good. But how could I do that? I couldn't leave the pupils and teachers to the mercy of that man.

I intended to find out more about Maligarth, and to do everything in my power to stop him.

Chapter 24

Still somewhat shocked by my experience at CASS, I magicked myself back to Washbridge, and made my way down the high street. As I did, I spotted a crowd of women outside Ever—they were carrying placards, and wearing the distinctive yellow uniforms of the Everettes.

As I got closer, I could see the wording on the placards. It read:

No more yellow. We are not canaries.

While walking around and around in a circle, they were chanting:

What do we want? No more yellow. When do we want it? Now.

"Hey, Julie," I called.

"Hi." She broke away from the protest, and came over to talk to me.

"What's going on?"

"We've had enough, Jill. The red outfits were bad enough, but we were prepared to put up with them. But these things." She gestured to the trouser suit. "They're beyond a joke."

"Have you tried talking to Grandma about them?"

"We've tried, yeah, but you more than anyone should know what she's like. There's no reasoning with her, so we've decided to withdraw our labour."

"When did that happen?"

"This morning. The final straw came when she handed out these." Julie fished something out of her pocket. "I mean, come on, I ask you." She put the yellow cap on her head just long enough to show me.

"That is pretty bad."

"We're not standing for it, Jill. Until she agrees to change back to the red, we're staying out here. We wouldn't even be averse to a nice shade of blue."

"Fair enough. I'm just on my way in to see her."

"Put a word in for us, would you?"

"I'll try, but I doubt anything I have to say will sway her."

If Grandma was worried by her staff's exodus, she certainly didn't show it. Sitting in her office, she was eating what looked like a Pot Noodle, except that the contents more closely resembled slugs.

Now I was just being ridiculous; no one would eat slugs.

"What's that you're eating, Grandma?"

"Pot Slug. Would you like some?"

"Err, no thanks, I'm good. I must say you seem to be taking all this very well."

"All what?"

"The Everettes going on strike."

"Is that what they're doing? I thought they were promoting the shop."

"They're protesting at having to wear the yellow uniforms."

"What's wrong with yellow? I like it."

"Yes, but *you* aren't the one who has to wear it. Couldn't you maybe—err—I don't know. Compromise, perhaps?"

She laughed. "That's very funny. Now, what did you want?"

"I need to ask your advice about something."

"Is it about your tweets?"

"Sorry?"

"I've read some of the rubbish you've been tweeting recently. Yawnsville. You're supposed to be creating a buzz, not sending people to sleep."

"I never know what to say in my tweets."

"Trust me, no one needs to know you've decided to wear your black flats. Who cares? Or that you're eating a blueberry muffin. As if that's news."

"I didn't come here to talk to you about my tweets."

"What is it then?" She picked up the carton, and poured the dregs down her throat. Just when I thought it couldn't get any more gross, she let out a huge burp that filled the room with the most revolting smell.

Struggling not to heave, I explained the situation at CASS.

"And what exactly do you expect me to do about it?" She grumbled.

"I thought you might have some advice on how I can find out more about Maligarth. If I knew who he was and where he came from, I'd at least know what I was up against. The problem is that no one knows anything about him."

"Tripe!" I thought for a horrible minute that she was calling for afters, but then she elaborated, "Utter tripe! I can think of someone who must know about him."

"Oh? Who?"

"He must have been appointed to that post by the governors of the school. I assume you've spoken to them?"

"Actually, I—err, no. I hadn't thought of that."

"Why would you? It's not like you're a P.I. or anything, is it?"

"You're right. That's what I'll do. I'll talk to the school governors."

As I left the shop, I was annoyed at myself for not having thought of something so obvious as contacting the governors. Maligarth hadn't just appeared out of thin air. He must have gone through some kind of vetting process. And yet, Desdemona Nightowl had said she knew nothing about him. Why hadn't the governors consulted her?

I intended to find out.

"Did you have any joy?" Julie said when I left the shop. "Were you able to make her see that we have a case?"

"Sorry. I really tried."

"Oh well, thanks anyway. The protest will go on, I guess."

I was just about to walk away when I noticed that the wording on the placards had changed. They each displayed a different message, some of which included:

Ever is the best!
Yellow Everettes love Ever!
Canaries Rule!

Unbelievable! Grandma had done it again.

***

As I was on my way back to the office, I spotted Deli.

"Hey, Deli, what happened to Betty's eyebrow?"

"Don't remind me. It's a nightmare."

"I feel bad about it because I was the one who recommended she go to your salon. I thought you'd set on an expert in eyebrow threading?"

"I did, but the awful woman received a better offer from another salon. We had no idea she wasn't going to join us until she called on the morning she was due to start."

"So who did Betty's eyebrows?"

"It was Nails. I wasn't in when he took the call from Fifi La Soux to say she wasn't coming in. If I had been, I'd have cancelled Betty's treatment. That stupid idiot decided he'd be able to do it himself."

"Had he ever done eyebrows before?"

"No, never. I could have killed him when I found out what had happened, but it was too late by then. Poor old Betty had only one eyebrow."

"She wasn't best pleased when I saw her. She was talking about suing you."

"I know, and to be honest, I wouldn't have blamed her if she had. I've talked to her since, and I've managed to get her to agree to a compromise. We're going to give her a free nail treatment every two weeks for a whole year, and I'm going to pencil in the missing eyebrow whenever she asks, for as long as it takes for it to grow back."

"And she's agreed to that, has she?"

"Yes, eventually. I originally offered free manicures for six months, but she insisted on a year. She's a tough cookie, that one."

"At least you've avoided legal action."

"Yeah, and it's not like the nail treatment is going to cost me anything. I'll be deducting it from Nails' allowance."

"You pay him an allowance?"

"It's the only way. The man is hopeless with money. If I let him have access to our bank account, we'd be bankrupt within a year."

"I'm surprised you bothered to offer to draw in her eyebrow."

"I hadn't intended to, but Betty pushed for that. She'd tried to do it herself, and let's just say, she's not the best."

"I'm pleased it all worked out. Anyway, I'd better get back to the office."

"Okay. See ya, Jill."

While I'd been at Ever, one of my signs had been removed as per my request.

There was just one slight problem.

"Mr Song's men came while you were out, Jill." Mrs V was just starting work on a new clown sock. "They've removed one of the signs."

"Yes, they have. The wrong one!"

"What?"

"They were supposed to remove the sign that says: Private Investigator, but they've removed the one that says: Jill Maxwell."

"Oh dear. I never thought to ask which sign they'd removed. I assumed they'd know which one to take down."

"I'm beginning to realise that when it comes to Sid Song, you can't assume anything."

"Are you going to give him a call?"

"I don't have the will or the energy. The replacement sign should be here within the next week or two. The one out there will just have to do until then."

"Very well, dear. I also took a call from the new office manager while you were out."

"Don't tell me he's changed his mind about taking the job?"

"No. In fact, he sounded very excited about starting here."

"Thank goodness for that. What did he want?"

"He asked about the dress code, and if there was any kind of canteen facility in the building. I told him smart casual, and that there wasn't a canteen, but there was a clown school."

"You did?"

"Yes, he seemed very interested in the clown school, so I took the opportunity to tell him that I'd be able to provide him with clown socks if he decided to enrol."

"Great."

What on earth would Alistair make of that conversation, I wondered. Hopefully, he wouldn't decide to bail on me like Fifi had done on Deli.

"Do you know what we need in this office?" Winky said.

"I bet you're going to tell me."

"A ball pool."

"And why would we need a ball pool?"

"They're brilliant for destressing after a busy day."

"When do you ever have a busy day?"

"It wouldn't just be for me. You could use it too."

"Thanks. That's very generous of you."

"And the new office manager. I bet she'd enjoy it."

"*She*? What makes you think it's a woman?"

"I heard you tell the old bag lady her name: Alice Stair."

"It's Alistair. One word."

"That's a disappointment. I was hoping for a pretty young thing to take Jules' place."

"You're out of luck, then."

"Still, I bet he'd enjoy the ball pool too."

"I'm not buying a ball pool, and that's final."

"I can remember when you used to be fun."

***

When I arrived home, there was a removal van at the house where the Makers had lived until recently.

"Hello, gorgeous." Jack came out of the kitchen to greet me.

"It looks like the new people are moving in across the road."

"I know. The removal van was here when I got home."

"Have you seen them yet?"

"No, not yet."

"Let's hope we get some normal people for a change. We're due some."

"The Livelys seem okay."

"They're both fitness freaks. There's nothing normal about that. What's for dinner?"

"I really fancy fish and chips. I thought we could have a walk to Never Battered. What do you say? Are you up for it?"

"Definitely, but this doesn't count as your turn for making dinner."

"I know. I'll make it tomorrow."

Whoever was moving into the Makers' old house certainly had a lot of furniture. That in itself was reassuring. The Makers had been nice enough people, but what they'd done to that house had been quite disturbing. Inside, it had resembled a factory rather than a residential property.

"Fish, chips and mushy peas twice," I said to Tish.

"Sorry. We aren't doing fish and chips anymore."

"Why not?"

"The soft furnishings really took off, so Chip and I decided to drop the food side of the business and focus on that."

"But you've still got the counter and the fryers? And the salt and vinegar."

"We're waiting for the shopfitters. We do have a great offer on ottomans this week if you're interested."

Chapter 25

"What do you look like?" I was doubled over with laughter.

"I don't see what's so funny," Jack said.

"You obviously haven't looked in the mirror, then."

"This is the recommended gear for sea fishing. I checked with the experts."

"Can you actually move in that suit?"

"Of course I can."

"It's enormous."

"It's a flotation suit."

"Those are the biggest gloves I've ever seen."

"They're very warm, though."

"Will you be able to hold the rod with those on?"

"I know what I'm doing."

"How much did this lot cost?"

"I didn't buy it. I hired it all from Cesar's Sea Fishing Emporium."

"What time is Peter coming?"

"He should be here any minute now." Jack tried to check his watch, but it was buried underneath his gloves and flotation suit. "What time are you meeting Kathy?"

"I'm going to pick her up at about ten. We'll do a bit of shopping, and then she's going to buy me lunch."

"Where are you going to eat?"

"We haven't decided yet." That wasn't true. I knew exactly where we'd be going, but I didn't want Jack to worry.

Just then, a car's horn sounded, so I went through to the lounge. "He's here."

As soon as Peter saw us walking down the driveway, he

dissolved into laughter too. "We're not going to the North Pole, mate."

"You'll be laughing on the other side of your face when you're frozen and I'm all snuggly and warm." Jack tried to climb into the passenger seat, but the suit was too bulky. "I'll get in the back."

"Look after him," I said to Peter.

***

I had some time to kill before I had to collect Kathy, so I took a walk to the corner shop because I was getting low on life's essentials.

"Just the custard creams today, Jill?" Little Jack seemed slightly taller than usual.

"Yeah, just these. Have you swapped your box?" I peered over the counter. "Stilts?"

"The box was rather limiting." He walked from one end of the counter to the other. "With these I can go anywhere in the shop."

"Aren't they a little dangerous? You could trip."

"Fear not, Jill. I undertook the Stilt Proficiency Course before I introduced them into the retail environment."

"Very sensible."

"It's fortuitous that you should come in this morning because our new shopping app goes live today."

"I wasn't sure you were serious about that."

"Deadly serious. It's adapt or die these days. I can install it on your phone now if you like, then you'll be good to go."

"Sure. Why not?" I passed him my phone.

"Okay. All done now." He held out the phone for me to

see. "That's it there. CornerShopTastic."

"Catchy name."

"Thanks. I came up with it after many hours of soul-searching. Give it a try the next time you're going to spend ten pounds or more."

"I'll do that, but how is Lucy going to cope with the increased demand for deliveries?"

"Once again, I would implore you to fret not. I have now employed an additional member of staff to assist with the deliveries. His name is Peter."

On my way back to the house, I came across a middle-aged couple walking towards me. They looked like a couple of bookends, dressed as they were in matching woolly jumpers, trousers and bobble hats. As they came closer, I noticed that their jumpers had a large letter 'N' on the front.

"Excuse me, young lady," the man said. "You wouldn't happen to know if there's a convenience store around here, would you?"

"Actually, I've just come from the corner shop. Carry on down this road, then take the second left."

"Thank you. We only moved into the area yesterday."

"I think we may be neighbours. Have you moved into the Makers' house?"

"We have indeed."

"I live across the road from you."

"We should introduce ourselves. We're the Normals."

"Thank goodness for that. I was only saying to Jack the other day that I hoped we got someone normal."

"Sorry?" They both shared the same puzzled look.

That's when the penny dropped. "You meant that your

name is Normal, didn't you?"

"Yes. I'm Norman, but everyone calls me Norm."

"Norm Normal?"

"Correct, and this is my wife, N—"

"Let me guess. Norma?"

"No. Naomi."

"Right. I'm Jill Maxwell, and my husband is Jack. He's gone sea fishing today."

"We like to play that fishing game with the magnetic fish, don't we, Naomi?"

"He always cheats." She had the weirdest laugh I'd ever heard. "Whenever we play, Norm puts a magnet in his pocket. He thinks I don't know, but I do."

"Right. Anyway, I should be making tracks."

"Did you know the Makers well, Jill?" Norm asked before I could escape.

"Not particularly. They weren't here for very long. His mother took ill, so they were forced to sell up."

"They've done some very strange things with the interior of the house. It's a good job I'm something of a handyman. There's a lot of work to be done."

"Right, I'd better get going."

"If you and your husband ever fancy a game of magnetic fishing, let us know."

"I'll definitely do that."

This could not be happening. If first impressions were anything to go by, the Normals were about as far from normal as it was possible to get. Just wait until I told Jack about this pair. No, scrub that idea. Knowing him, he'd want to organise a magnetic fishing tournament.

***

The arrangement was that Kathy would be ready and waiting when I arrived at her house, but when I pulled up outside there was no sign of her. I tooted the horn but to no avail.

Typical. She'd always been the same.

I knocked on the door and let myself in. "Hello?" There was no reply, but I could hear music coming from upstairs. "Kathy!"

It was useless, she'd never hear me over that noise.

I found her in the bedroom, trying on clothes in front of the mirror. When she spotted me, she said something, but I couldn't make out what she'd said.

"I can't hear you for the music," I shouted.

She turned it down. "What did you say?"

"I said I couldn't—never mind."

"What do you think? This one?" She did a twirl in the red dress. "Or this one?" She picked up the blue dress from the bed and held it in front of her.

"Either. They're both nice. I thought we agreed I'd pick you up at ten?"

"What time is it?"

"Five past."

"Sorry. Pete's parents kept me talking, so I haven't had long to decide what to wear."

"We're only going shopping."

"And for lunch."

"Actually, that reminds me. Would you mind if we had lunch at Liberty's?"

"It's ages since I was in there. In fact, I think the last time was on my birthday. Do you remember?"

"That day is a bit of a blur."

"For me too." She laughed. "I seem to remember you had to bring me home."

"I'd forgotten about that." I hadn't. In fact, I still felt a twinge of guilt about that day because I'd convinced Kathy she'd been drunk, when in fact I'd actually used the 'sleep' spell on her.

"Isn't Liberty's more of a bar?"

"They do food too. To be honest, I'm working on a case, and there's a guy who works there that I need to check out."

"What kind of case?"

"Murder."

"How exciting! Did I ought to wear something more sleuth-like?"

"That won't be necessary."

"I could wear dark glasses and a big hat."

"Please don't."

"Will you need me to create a diversion?"

I was already beginning to regret this.

Three hours later, and I'd remembered why I never went shopping with Kathy. The woman was relentless. I'd thought the young assistant in the shoe shop was going to throttle her after Kathy tried on twenty-three pairs of shoes, only to walk out empty-footed. Think I'm joking? I wish I was. And don't get me started on the perfume department.

"I'm starving," I said while trying to pull her away from yet another perfume sampler.

"What do you think of this one?" She offered me her wrist to smell.

"It's fantastic. Much like the last twenty-two you've tried. Now, can we please get some lunch?"

"You've never had the shopping gene, have you, Jill?"

"Apparently not. Listen, this is important. When we get to the bar, you have to act naturally. Okay?"

"Act naturally. Got it. By the way, I did slip my dark glasses into my bag, just in case."

"Great."

As soon as we walked into Liberty's, I spotted Duncan's distinctive curly hair. He and two young women were busy behind the bar.

Mainly because I was afraid of what Kathy might do, I found us a table as far away from the bar as possible.

"What's the plan?" she said from behind the menu.

"To order food, but it might help if you held the menu the right way up."

"Right, sorry. This is exciting, isn't it? Who is it you're checking up on?"

"Do you see the guy with curly hair behind the bar?"

"Yeah. Is he the murderer?"

"Shush!"

"Sorry."

"Stay right here while I go and order the drinks and food. I may be a while because I'm going to flirt with him."

"Flirt?" She laughed. "You?"

"What's so funny about that?"

"You've never been able to flirt."

"Of course I can flirt."

"You used to send me to ask the boys if they liked you."

"That was when I was ten. Don't move from this seat,

and don't do anything to draw attention to yourself. Got it?"

"Check."

"Okay." I stood up and started towards the bar.

I'd only gone a few feet when —

"Jill! Wait!"

I hurried back to the table. "I thought I told you not to draw attention to yourself."

"You didn't ask what I want to eat or drink."

"Oh yeah, sorry."

Once I had Kathy's order, I made my way over to the bar, making sure to stand in the section that Duncan was covering.

"Yes, love. What can I get for you?"

"Hello, handsome. What did you have in mind?"

What do you mean that was a pathetic attempt at flirting? I was a bit rusty. Sheesh, you lot are so judgemental.

"I meant what would you like to drink?"

"Sorry, I was a little distracted by your good looks. I love a man with curly hair."

"Really?" He grinned. Bait taken. "Maybe we could get a drink when I get off in an hour."

"I'd love to, but I'm with my sister at the moment." I gestured towards Kathy who must have seen me because she put on her dark glasses and hid behind the menu again. "She's a bit of a drag."

"What about this evening?" He leaned a little closer. "I'm not working tonight."

"Sure. I'd like that. I have an apartment close to the canal. We could go for a walk, grab a drink and then maybe go back to my place."

"Sounds good."

After finalising the arrangements for our 'date', and placing our order, I returned to Kathy who was still wearing the dark glasses.

"You can take those off now."

"Are you sure? I thought he'd spotted me."

"Yeah, it's perfectly safe. Mission accomplished. You can call me the queen of flirt."

***

If I'd thought the morning's shopping had been bad, it paled into insignificance compared to what I was forced to endure in the afternoon. By the time we headed back to the car, we were both weighed down with carrier bags.

All of which belonged to Kathy.

I'd bought a toothbrush and a pair of Odor Eaters.

"What will Peter say when he sees how much you've spent?" I said while trying to fit all the bags into the boot of my car.

"He won't mind."

"How can you be so sure?"

"Because by the time he gets home, this lot will all be in my wardrobe and he won't realise they're new."

"You're so devious. What about when the credit card bill arrives?"

"I handle all the household money."

"That's a scary thought."

"We're doing okay financially now that both of our businesses are thriving. I wonder how the guys are doing?"

"I just hope Peter hasn't caught too many fish. If Jack's got a drubbing, I'll never hear the end of it. He's such a bad loser."

"Unlike you, obviously."

"I never lose, so the question never arises."

Chapter 26

I'd never seen that particular shade of green before. Not until Jack arrived home from his sea fishing expedition. Peter had to help him up the drive.

"Let me die," Jack groaned.

"He's been like this from the moment the boat set sail." Peter grinned.

"I'm going to be sick."

Between the two of us, Peter and I managed to get Jack into the bathroom where we left him kneeling next to the toilet.

"I take it he didn't catch many fish?"

"Not one. He spent most of the time lying down or being sick."

"What about you? You seem okay."

"I had a great time. I caught eleven whoppers."

Meanwhile, if the sounds coming from the bathroom were anything to go by, Jack was not having such a good time.

"Thanks for getting him home, Peter. I'll take it from here."

"What about you and Kathy? Did you buy much?"

"*I* didn't."

"I assume that means my darling wife did?"

"I couldn't possibly comment."

Snigger.

About half an hour after Peter had left, Jack finally emerged from the bathroom.

"I take it you didn't win the fishing bet?" I quipped.

"I'm not in the mood, Jill. I'm going to bed."

"I was just about to make myself a fry-up. Do you fancy one?"

He put his hand over his mouth and rushed back to the bathroom.

***

By the time I left for my 'date' with Duncan, Jack was in bed, sound asleep. I didn't bother trying to tell him where I was going, but I did leave him a note in case he woke up and wondered where I was.

I arrived at the canal thirty minutes early because there was something I needed to do before Duncan got there. The Green Lady was still moored in the same spot where I'd left her after my precarious trip downstream. I had to make sure I got this just right, so I spent some considerable time checking I had the angles correct.

Once I was satisfied, I jumped off the boat, and walked upstream to the point where I'd arranged to meet Duncan.

The man might be a murderer, but he was punctual. And by the look of it, he'd spent quite some time getting spruced up for his date with little old me.

"Hi, gorgeous!" He beamed, as he walked towards me. "You're even more beautiful than I remember."

"It's only been a few hours since you saw me."

"Where would you like to go for a drink?"

"Actually, I've changed my mind about that."

"How about we go straight to your apartment instead, then?"

"No, I meant I'd changed my mind about all of this."

"What do you mean?"

"I've just recently split up with my boyfriend."

"So? I'll soon make you forget about him."

"That's just it. I don't want to forget about him. I still love him very much and I want to give it another chance. I'm sorry. You do understand, don't you?"

"I understand that you're a little tease." He spat the words. "Do you get off on messing guys around like this?"

"It isn't like that." I turned around and began to walk away.

"Where do you think you're going? You can't drag me here and then just leave."

"I'm sorry." I picked up my pace.

"Come here. We're not done." He began to follow me.

I ran along the towpath, and didn't stop until I was level with The Green Lady. Then I turned to face him.

"Do you remember this boat, Duncan?"

"I don't know what you're talking about."

It was obvious he did because he'd stopped dead in his tracks as soon as he'd seen it.

"Take a closer look. This used to belong to a young woman named Pam Turton, but you already know that. You've been on board it, haven't you?"

"I have no idea what you're talking about. Who are you, anyway?"

"Did she reject your advances?"

"This is nonsense."

"You don't take rejection well, do you, Duncan? I heard how you beat up a guy just because he had the nerve to talk to the woman you were with."

"That's a lie."

"I've seen the photograph of Pam and her ex that you smashed. I imagine it will have your fingerprints all over it."

"Shut up! I don't have to listen to this nonsense!"

"What happened? Did you hit her and then push her body into the water? You're a pathetic little man who takes out his insecurity on helpless women."

He glanced around. "Whoever you are, you've messed with the wrong man this time."

"What are you going to do? Kill me, just like you killed Pam?"

"That's exactly what I'm going to do."

He lunged forward, but I easily avoided his attempts to grab me. Then, I edged slowly backwards until I hit my mark. Once I was there, I cast the 'power' spell, and waited for him to come at me again. This time when he tried to grab me, I caught him under the chin with an uppercut that felled him.

***

"Who's this?" Sue Shay demanded when she and two uniformed officers arrived on the scene.

Duncan was lying at my feet, bound hand and foot. He'd come around a few minutes before the police arrived.

"As I told your colleague on the phone, this is Pam Turton's murderer."

"I want this woman arrested for assault," Duncan shouted.

Sue Shay grabbed me by the arm and frogmarched me a few yards down the towpath. "What's going on,

Maxwell?"

"Well done on remembering my name."

"We already have the murderer in custody."

"Actually, you don't. Radford is a burglar, and what he did to my PA is unforgiveable, but he didn't murder Pam Turton."

"And what proof do you have that this man did?"

"How about his confession on video?"

She looked around. "There's no CCTV on this stretch of the canal."

"You're right. And that's precisely why Duncan was prepared to attack me, just like he did to Pam. He assumed because there were no cameras that he'd get away with it again." I took out my phone. "Except, that this time he was wrong." I played her the video that I'd recorded a few minutes earlier.

She turned back to the uniformed officers. "Take this man away." Once they'd carried out her orders, she said to me, "I'm going to need to hang onto this phone."

"Be my guest."

She played the video again. "How did you manage to overpower him?"

"He tripped and banged his head."

"Hmm. How very convenient for you that he waited until he was out of shot before tripping."

***

The next morning, Jack was still feeling very delicate.

"Come on, Jack. It's Sunday. I thought we could take a drive out later and get lunch somewhere nice."

"I can't. I still feel like death warmed up."

"That's just great. What am I supposed to do by myself all day?"

"I'm sorry. I'll make it up to you next weekend."

"By the way, I caught the real murderer in the Pam Turton case last night."

"That's nice. Can you turn the light out, please? It's hurting my eyes."

Fantastic! I'd spent all Saturday being dragged around the shops by Kathy, and now I looked like spending Sunday on my lonesome.

With nothing better to do, I spent the morning bingeing on TV box sets. I'd checked on Jack a couple of times in the hope that he might have come around, but he'd been dead to the world.

By midday, I was starving and would have killed for a big Sunday lunch, but it looked like being a Pot Noodle for me.

Just then, my phone rang.

"Jill? It's Daze. I'm sorry to bother you on a Sunday. Is there any chance you could come over?"

"Right now?"

"Yes, please. It's really urgent."

"What's happened?"

"It'd be better if I explain when you get here. We're in Candlefield Community Centre."

"Okay. I'll be there in a couple of minutes."

***

"Surprise!"

What the—?

I'd just set foot inside the community centre when several dozen witches, who I'd never seen before in my life, started clapping and cheering. I would probably have thought I had the wrong address if it hadn't been for the large banner draped across the centre of the room. It read:

Thank you, Jill Maxwell.

I had absolutely no idea what was going on.

"Sorry for the subterfuge, Jill." Daze appeared at my side.

"What's this all about? If you think it's my birthday, you've got the wrong date."

"It's a surprise party to say thank you."

"For what? And who are all these women? I don't know any of them."

"These are the witches who were taken back to Candlefield by Royston Rhodes. They'd all been duped by the dating agency, which we now know was run by his wife. Because of the exceptional circumstances, the authorities have agreed that they can all return to their husbands in the human world."

"That's fantastic, but how are they going to do that? Their husbands know they're witches now."

"In view of the scale of the miscarriage of justice that took place, several level six witches were asked to come up with a spell that will ensure that particular memory is erased from the minds of these ladies' husbands. There may be a few awkward questions about where they've been, but the feeling is that their partners will be so pleased to have them back, that will soon be forgotten."

"That's really great news. I'm delighted for them."

"So you see, Jill, that's why they wanted to throw this party for you. And they're not the only ones who are in your debt. Without your help I probably wouldn't be a rogue retriever today." She handed me a huge box of chocolates. "This is just a small token of my appreciation."

"There really was no need."

"We're not done yet."

At that moment, a dozen floral fairies led by Butter, flew into the room.

"This is for you, Jill." Butter handed me a single red rose. "For saving our water supply."

Before I could thank her, the other fairies all took it in turns to hand me their roses.

It's not often that I'm lost for words, but I was choked, and close to tears.

"Okay, guys!" Daze shouted. "Bring on the food."

From a door to my left, the twins, Mindy and several other witches appeared. They were pushing trollies stacked full of all manner of delicious sandwiches, cakes and desserts.

Result!

***

Aunt Lucy had been looking after her granddaughters at her house, but she'd brought them to join us for the last half hour of the celebrations.

"More cake, Jill?"

"Not for me, thanks. I couldn't possibly eat another bite."

"It was a wonderful thing you did, re-uniting these witches with their partners."

"I can't take all the credit for that, but I am glad I was able to bring Rhodes to justice if only for Daze's sake. If anyone should head that department, it's her."

"I hear you've been helping the floral fairies again too."

"Yeah, but that was more luck than judgement. If the head zookeeper hadn't come to me because he was worried about the Woolly Massives, I might never have got to the bottom of the water supply shortages."

"What's Jack up to today?"

"He's not feeling too good. He and Peter went sea fishing yesterday. When he came home, he was a funny shade of green."

"Poor darling. You ought to get back home to look after him."

"Judging by how he was first thing this morning, I doubt very much he'll even be out of bed yet."

It turned out I was wrong.

"Jack? You're up?"

"I'm feeling so much better." He looked it too; the colour was back in his cheeks.

"That's good."

"I'm starving; I haven't eaten since yesterday morning. I thought we could go out for Sunday lunch."

"You're stone out of luck. I'm absolutely stuffed."

"I didn't think you would have eaten yet."

I told him all about the surprise party in Candlefield, and all the delicious food that I'd devoured.

"In that case, I suppose I'd better knock myself something up for lunch."

"There's fish in the freezer."

ALSO BY ADELE ABBOTT

The Witch P.I. Mysteries
(A Candlefield/Washbridge Series)

Witch Is When... (Books #1 to #12)
Witch Is When It All Began
Witch Is When Life Got Complicated
Witch Is When Everything Went Crazy
Witch Is When Things Fell Apart
Witch Is When The Bubble Burst
Witch Is When The Penny Dropped
Witch Is When The Floodgates Opened
Witch Is When The Hammer Fell
Witch Is When My Heart Broke
Witch Is When I Said Goodbye
Witch Is When Stuff Got Serious
Witch Is When All Was Revealed

Witch Is Why... (Books #13 to #24)
Witch Is Why Time Stood Still
Witch is Why The Laughter Stopped
Witch is Why Another Door Opened
Witch is Why Two Became One
Witch is Why The Moon Disappeared
Witch is Why The Wolf Howled
Witch is Why The Music Stopped
Witch is Why A Pin Dropped
Witch is Why The Owl Returned
Witch is Why The Search Began
Witch is Why Promises Were Broken
Witch is Why It Was Over

Witch Is How... (Books #25 to #36)
Witch is How Things Had Changed
Witch is How Berries Tasted Good
Witch is How The Mirror Lied
Witch is How The Tables Turned
Witch is How The Drought Ended
Witch is How The Dice Fell
Witch is How The Biscuits Disappeared
Witch is How Dreams Became Reality
Witch is How Bells Were Saved
Witch is How To Fool Cats
Witch is How To Lose Big
Witch is How Life Changed Forever

Susan Hall Investigates
(A Candlefield/Washbridge Series)
Whoops! Our New Flatmate Is A Human.
Whoops! All The Money Went Missing.
Whoops! Someone Is On Our Case.
Whoops! We're In Big Trouble Now.

Web site: AdeleAbbott.com
Facebook: facebook.com/AdeleAbbottAuthor
Instagram: #adele_abbott_author

Made in the USA
Monee, IL
15 June 2023

35847927R00156